Books by Dick Francis

Blood Sport
Bonecrack
Dead Cert
Enquiry
Flying Finish
For Kicks
Forfeit
High Stakes
In the Frame
Knockdown
Nerve
Odds Against
Rat Race
Risk
Slayride
Smokescreen

Published by POCKET BOOKS

Dick Francis

Rat Race

PUBLISHED BY POCKET BOOKS NEW YORK

POCKET BOOKS, a Simon & Schuster division of
GULF & WESTERN CORPORATION
1230 Avenue of the Americas, New York, N.Y. 10020

ISBN: 0-671-82158-X

First Pocket Books printing December, 1978

10   9   8   7   6   5   4   3   2

Trademarks registered in the United States and other countries.

Printed in the U.S.A.

Chapter One

I picked four of them up at White Waltham in the new Cherokee Six 300 that never got a chance to grow old. The pale blue upholstery still had a new leather smell and there wasn't a scratch on the glossy white fuselage. A nice little airplane, while it lasted.

They had ordered me for noon but they were already in the bar when I landed at eleven-forty. Three double whiskies and a lemonade.

Identification was easy: several chairs around a small table were draped with four lightweight raincoats, three binocular cases, two copies of *Sporting Life* and one lightweight racing saddle. The four passengers were standing nearby in the sort of spread-about group indicative of people thrown together by business rather than natural friendship. They were not talking to each other, though it looked as though they had been. One, a large man, had a face full of anger. The smallest, evidently a jockey, was flushed and rigid. Two others, an elderly man and a middle-aged woman, were steadfastly staring at nothing in particular in the way that meant a lot of furious activity was going on inside their heads.

I walked toward them across the large lounge-reception room and spoke to an indeterminate spot in midair.

"Major Tyderman?"

The elderly man who said "Yes?" had been made a major a good long time ago. Nearer seventy than sixty; but still with a tough little body, wiry little mustache, sharp little eyes. He had thin salt-and-pepper hair brushed sideways across a balding crown and he carried his head stiffly, with his chin tucked back into his neck. Tense: very tense. And wary, looking at the world with suspicion.

He wore a lightweight speckled fawn suit vaguely reminiscent in cut of his military origins, and, unlike the others, had not parked his binoculars but wore them with the strap diagonally across his chest and the case facing forward on his stomach, like a sporran. Club badges of metal and colored cardboard hung in thick clusters at each side.

"Your airplane is here, Major," I said. "I'm Matt Shore. . . . I'm flying you."

He glanced over my shoulder, looking for someone else.

"Where's Larry?" he asked abruptly.

"He left," I said. "He got a job in Turkey."

The Major's gaze came back from the search with a click. "You're new," he said accusingly.

"Yes," I agreed.

"I hope you know the way."

He meant it seriously. I said politely, "I'll do my best."

The second of the passengers, the woman on the Major's left, said flatly, "The last time I flew to the races, the pilot got lost."

I looked at her, giving her my best approximation to a confidence-boosting smile. "The weather's good enough today not to have any fear of it."

It wasn't true. There were cu-nims forecast for the June afternoon. And anyone can get lost anytime if enough goes wrong. The woman on the left of Major Tyderman gave me a disillusioned stare and I stopped wasting my confidence builder. She didn't need it. She had all the confidence in the world. She was fifty and fragile-looking, with graying hair cut in a straight-across fringe and a jaw-length bob. There were two mild brown eyes under heavy dark eyebrows and a mouth that looked gentle; yet she held

2

herself and behaved with the easy authority of a much higher command than the Major's. She was the only one of the group not outwardly ruffled.

The Major had been looking at his watch. "You're early," he said. "We've got time for the other half." He turned to the barman and ordered refills, and as an afterthought said to me, "Something for you?"

I shook my head. "No, thank you."

The woman said indifferently, "No alcohol for eight hours before a flight. Isn't that the rule?"

"More or less," I agreed.

The third passenger, the large angry-looking man, morosely watched the barman push the measure up twice on the Johnnie Walker. "Eight hours. Good God," he said. He looked as if eight hours seldom passed for him without topping up. The bulbous nose, the purple thread veins on his cheeks, the swelling paunch—they had all cost a lot in excise duty.

The atmosphere I had walked into slowly subsided. The jockey sipped his low-calorie lemonade, and the bright pink flush faded from his cheekbones and came out in fainter mottles on his neck. He seemed about twenty-one or two, reddish-haired, with a naturally small frame and a moist-looking skin. Few weight problems, I thought. No dehydration. Fortunate for him.

The Major and his large friend drank rapidly, muttered unintelligibly, and removed themselves to the Gents. The woman eyed the jockey and said in a voice which sounded more friendly than her comment, "Are you out of your mind, Kenny Bayst? If you go on antagonizing Major Tyderman, you'll be looking for another job."

The jockey flicked his eyes to me and away again, compressing his rosebud mouth. He put the half-finished lemonade on the table and picked up one of the raincoats and the racing saddle.

"Which plane?" he said to me. "I'll stow my gear."

He had a strong Australian accent with a resentful bite to it. The woman watched him with what would have passed for a smile but for the frost in her eyes.

3

"The baggage door is locked," I said. "I'll come over with you." To the woman I said, "Can I carry your coat?"

"Thank you." She indicated the coat which was obviously hers, a shiny rust-colored affair with copper buttons. I picked it up, and also the businesslike binoculars lying on top, and followed the jockey out of the door.

After ten fuming paces, he said explosively, "It's too damn easy to blame the man on top."

"They always blame the pilot," I said mildly. "Fact of life."

"Huh?" he said. "Oh, yeah. Too right. They do."

We reached the end of the path and started across the grass. He was still oozing grudge. I wasn't much interested.

"For the record," I said, "what are the names of my other passengers? Besides the Major, that is."

He turned his head in surprise. "Don't you know her? Our Annie Villars? Looks like someone's cozy old granny and has a tongue that would flay a kangaroo. Everyone knows our little Annie." His tone was sour and disillusioned.

"I don't know much about racing," I said.

"Oh? Well, she's a trainer, then. A damned good trainer, I'll say that for her. I wouldn't stay with her else. Not with that tongue of hers. I'll tell you, sport, she can roust her stable lads out on the gallops in words a sergeant major never thought of. But sweet as milk with the owners. Has them eating out of her little hand."

"The horses, too?"

"Uh? Oh, yeah. The horses love her. She can ride like a jock, too, when she's a mind to. Not that she does it much now. She must be getting on a bit. Still, she knows what she's at, true enough. She knows what a horse can do and what it can't, and that's most of the battle in this game."

His voice held resentment and admiration in roughly equal amounts.

4

I said, "What is the name of the other man? The big one."

This time it was pure resentment: no admiration. He spat the name out syllable by deliberate syllable, curling his lips away from his teeth.

"Mr. Eric Goldenberg."

Having got rid of the name, he shut his mouth tight and was clearly taking his employer's remarks to heart. We reached the aircraft and stowed the coats and his saddle in the baggage space behind the rear seats.

"We're going to Newbury first, aren't we?" he asked. "To pick up Colin Ross?"

"Yes."

He gave me a sardonic look. "Well, you *must* have heard of Colin Ross."

"I guess," I said, "that I have."

It would have been difficult not to, since the champion jockey was twice as popular as the Prime Minister and earned six times as much. His face appeared on half the billboards in Britain encouraging the populace to drink more milk, and his sharp wits convulsed the headlines at least once a month. There was even a picture strip about him in a children's comic. Everyone, but everyone, had heard of Colin Ross.

Kenny Bayst climbed in through the rear-end door and sat in one of the two rear seats. I took a quick look round the outside of the aircraft, even though I'd done a thorough preflight check on it not an hour before, when I left base. It was my first week, my fourth day, my third flight for Derrydowns Sky Taxis, and after the way fate had clobbered me in the past, I was taking no chances.

There were no nuts loose, no rivets missing on the sharp-nosed little six-seater. There were eight quarts of oil where there should have been eight quarts of oil, there were no dead birds clogging up the air intakes to the engine, there were no punctures in the tires, no cracks in the green or red glass over navigation lights, no chips in the propeller blades, no loose radio aerials. The pale blue cowling over the engine

5

was securely clipped down, and the matching pale blue cowling over the struts and wheels of the fixed undercarriage were as solid as rocks.

By the time I'd finished, the other three passengers were coming across the grass. Goldenberg was doing the talking with steam still coming out of his ears, while the Major nodded agreement in unhappy little jerks and Annie Villars looked as if she wasn't listening. When they arrived within earshot, Goldenberg was saying ". . . can't lay the horse unless we're sure he'll pull it—" But he stopped short when the Major gestured sharply in my direction. He need hardly have bothered. I had no curiosity about their affairs.

On the principle that in a light aircraft it is better to have the center of gravity as far forward as possible, I asked Goldenberg to sit in front in the right-hand seat beside me, and put the Major and Annie Villars in the center two seats, and left Kenny in one of the last two, with the empty one ready for Colin Ross. The four rear seats were reached by the port-side door, but Goldenberg had to climb in by stepping up on the low wing on the starboard side and lowering himself into his seat through the forward door. He waited while I got in before him and moved over to my side, then squeezed his bulk in through the door and settled heavily into his seat.

They were all old hands at air taxis: they had their safety belts fastened before I did mine, and when I looked round to check that they were ready to go, the Major was already deep in *Sporting Life*. Kenny Bayst was cleaning his nails with fierce little jabs, relieving his frustration by hurting himself.

I got clearance from the tower and lifted the little airplane away for the twenty-mile hop across Berkshire. Taxi flying was a lot different from the airlines, and finding racecourses looked more difficult to me than being radar-vectored into Heathrow. I'd never before flown a racecourse trip, and I'd asked my predecessor Larry about it that morning when he'd come into the office to collect his cards.

"Newbury's a cinch," he said offhandedly. "Just

6

point its nose at that vast runway the Yanks built at
Greenham Common. You can practically see it from
Scotland. The racecourse is just north of it, and the
landing strip is parallel with the white rails of the
finishing straight. You can't miss it. Good long strip.
No problems. As for Haydock, it's just where the M6
motorway crosses the East Lancs road. Piece of cake."

He took himself off to Turkey, stopping on one foot
at the doorway for some parting advice. "You'll have
to practice short landings before you go to Bath; and
avoid Yarmouth in a heat wave. It's all yours now,
mate, and the best of British Luck."

It was true that you could see Greenham Common
from a long way off, but on a fine day it would
anyway have been difficult to lose the way from
White Waltham to Newbury: the main railway line to
Exeter ran more or less straight from one to the other.
My passengers had all flown into Newbury before,
and the Major helpfully told me to look out for the
electric cables strung across the approach. We landed
respectably on the newly mown grass and taxied
along the strip toward the grandstand end, braking to
a stop just before the boundary fence.

Colin Ross wasn't there.

I shut down the engine, and in the sudden silence
Annie Villars remarked, "He's bound to be late. He
said he was riding work for Bob Smith, and Bob's
never on time getting his horses out."

The other three nodded vaguely, but they were
still not on ordinarily chatty terms with one another,
and after about five minutes of heavy silence I asked
Goldenberg to let me out to stretch my legs. He
grunted and mumbled at having to climb out onto the
wing to let me past him, and I gathered I was breaking Derrydowns' Number 1 rule: never annoy the
customers; you're going to need them again.

Once I was out of their company, however, they
did start talking. I walked round to the front of
the aircraft and leaned against the leading edge of the
wing, and looked up at the scattered clouds in the blue-
gray sky and thought unprofitably about this and that.

7

Behind me their voices rose acrimoniously, and when they opened the door wide to get some air, scraps of what they were saying floated across.

". . . simply asking for a dope test." Annie Villars.

". . . if you can't ride a losing race better than last time . . . find someone else." Goldenberg.

". . . very difficult position . . ." Major Tyderman.

A short sharp snap from Kenny, and Annie Villars' exasperated exclamation. "Bayst!"

". . . not paying you more than last time." The Major, very emphatically.

Indistinct protest from Kenny, and a violently clear reaction from Goldenberg: "Bugger your license."

Kenny, my lad, I thought remotely, if you don't watch out you'll end up like me, still with a license but with not much else.

A Ford-of-all-work rolled down the road past the grandstands, came through the gate in the boundary fence, and bounced over the turf toward the aircraft. It stopped about twenty feet away, and two men climbed out. The larger, who had been driving, went round to the back and pulled out a brown canvas-and-leather overnight grip. The smaller one walked on over the grass. I took my weight off the wing and stood up. He stopped a few paces away, waiting for the larger man to catch up. He was dressed in faded blue jeans and a whitish cotton sweat shirt with navy-blue edgings. Black canvas shoes on his narrow feet. He had nondescript brownish hair over an exceptionally broad forehead, a short straight nose, and a delicate feminine-looking chin. All his bones were fine and his waist and hips would have been the despair of Victorian maidens. Yet there was something unmistakably masculine about him: and more than that, he was mature. He looked at me with the small still smile behind the eyes which is the hallmark of those who know what life is really about. His soul was old. He was twenty-six.

"Good morning," I said.

He held out his hand, and I shook it. His clasp was cool, firm, and brief.

"No Larry?" he inquired.

"He's left. I'm Matt Shore."

"Fine," he said noncommittally. He didn't introduce himself. He knew there was no need. I wondered what it was like to be in that position. It hadn't affected Colin Ross. He had none of the "I am" aura which often clings around the notably successful, and from the extreme understatement of his clothes I gathered that he avoided it consciously.

"We're late, I'm afraid," he said. "Have to bend the throttle."

"Do my best. . . ."

The larger man arrived with the grip, and I stowed it in the forward luggage locker between the engine wall and the forward bulkhead of the cabin. By the time the baggage door was securely fastened, Colin Ross had found his empty seat and strapped himself into it. Goldenberg, with heavy grunts, moved out again so that I could get back to my left-hand place. The larger man, who was apparently the dilatory trainer Bob Smith, said his hellos and goodbyes to the passengers, and stood watching afterward while I started the engine and taxied back to the other end of the strip to turn into wind for takeoff.

The flight north was uneventful: I went up the easy way under the Amber 1 airway, navigating on the radio beacons at Daventry, Lichfield, and Oldham. Manchester control routed us right round the north of their zone, so that I had to drop down southward toward Haydock racecourse, and there it was, just as Larry had said, near the interchange of the two giant roads. We touched down on the grass strip indicated in the center of the course, and I taxied on and parked where the Major told me to, near the rails of the track itself, a mere hundred yards from the grandstand.

The passengers disembarked themselves and their belongings and Colin Ross looked at his watch. A faint smile hovered and was gone. He made no comment. He said merely, "Are you coming in to the races?"

I shook my head. "Think I'll stay over here."

9

"I'll arrange with the man on the gate to let you into the paddock, if you change your mind."

"Thanks," I said in surprise. "Thanks very much."

He nodded briefly and set off without waiting for the others, ducking under the white-painted rails and trudging across the track.

"Pilots' perks," Kenny said, taking his raincoat from my hand and putting his arm forward for the saddle. "You want to take advantage."

"Maybe I will," I said, but I didn't mean to. Horse racing began and ended with the Derby as far as I was concerned, and also I was a non-gambler by nature.

Annie Villars said in her deceptively gentle voice, "You do understand that we're all going on to Newmarket after the races, and not back to Newbury?"

"Yes," I assured her. "That's what I was told."

"Good."

"If we don't go to jail," Kenny said under his breath. Goldenberg looked at me sharply to see if I'd heard that, and I gave no sign of it. Whatever they were about, it was as little my concern as who killed Cock Robin.

Major Tyderman pushed at his mustache with a hand rigid with nervous energy and said, "Last race at four-thirty. Need a drink after that. Ready to start back at, say, five-fifteen. That all right with you?"

"Perfectly, Major." I nodded.

"Right," he said. "Good." His gaze was flicking from one to another of his traveling companions, assessing and suspicious. His eyes narrowed fiercely at Kenny Bayst, opened and narrowed again rapidly on Goldenberg, relaxed on Annie Villars, and went cold on the vanishing back of Colin Ross. The thoughts behind the outward physical reactions were unguessable, and when he finally looked back at me he didn't really see me; he was busy with the activity inside his head.

"Five-fifteen," he repeated vaguely. "Good."

Kenny said to me, "Don't waste your money in the three-thirty, sport," and Goldenberg raised his fist, his face going purple with anger, and nearly hit him.

Annie Villars' voice rapped into him, the steel sticking through the cream with a vengeance, the top-brass quality transcendent and withering.

"Control yourself, you stupid man."

Goldenberg's mouth literally dropped open, to reveal a bottom row of unappetizing brown-stained teeth. His raised fist lowered slowly, and he looked altogether foolish.

"As for you," she said to Kenny, "I told you to keep your tongue still, and that was your last chance."

"Are you sacking me?" he asked.

"I'll decide that at the end of the afternoon."

Kenny showed no anxiety about keeping his job, and I realized that in fact what he had been doing was trying to provoke them into getting rid of him. He'd got himself into nutcrackers and while they squeezed he couldn't get out.

I became mildly curious to see what would happen in the three-thirty. It would help to pass the afternoon.

They straggled off toward the stands, Kenny in front, the Major and Goldenberg together, with Annie Villars several paces behind. The Major kept stopping and looking back and waiting for her, but each time just as she reached him he turned and went off again in front, so that as a piece of courtesy the whole thing was wasted. He reminded me vividly of an aunt who had taken me for childhood walks in just that way. I remembered quite clearly that it had been infuriating.

I sighed, shut the baggage doors, and tidied up the airplane. Annie Villars had been smoking thin brown cigars. Goldenberg had been eating indigestion tablets, each from a square wrapper. The Major had left his *Sporting Life* in a tumbled heap on the floor.

While I was fiddling around with the debris, two more airplanes flew in, a four-seat high-winged Cessna and a six-seat twin-engined Aztec.

I watched their touchdowns with an uncritical eye, though I wouldn't have given the Aztec pilot a gold medal for his double bounce. Several small men disgorged themselves and made a dart like a flock of starlings across the track toward the paddock. They were followed by three or four larger and slower-moving people, slung around with binoculars and what I later learned to be bags for carrying sets of racing colors. Finally out of each aircraft popped the most leisurely of all the inmates, a man dressed very much as I was, in dark trousers, white shirt, neat dark tie.

They strolled toward each other and lit cigarettes. After a while, not wanting to seem unsociable, I wandered across to join them. They turned and watched me come, but with no welcome in unsmiling faces. "Hello," I said moderately. "Nice day."

"Perhaps," said one.

"You think so?" said the other.

They offered me fish-eyed stares but no cigarette. I had grown hardened to that sort of thing. I turned half away from them to read the names of the firms they flew for, which were painted on the tails of their aircraft. It was the same name on both. Polyplane Services.

How dreary of them, I thought, to be so antagonistic. I gave them the benefit of a very small doubt and made one more approach.

"Have you come far?"

They didn't answer. Just gave me the stares, like two cod.

I laughed at them as if I thought their behavior pathetic, which in fact I did, and turned on my heel to go back to my own territory. When I'd gone several steps, one of them called after me, "Where's Larry Gedge?" He didn't sound as if he liked Larry any better than me.

I decided not to hear: if they really wanted to know, they could come and ask nicely. It was their turn to cross the grass.

They didn't bother. I wasn't particularly sorry. I had long ago learned that pilots were not all one great happy brotherhood. Pilots could be as bloody-minded to each other as any group on earth.

I climbed back into my seat in the Cherokee and

sorted out my maps and flight plans for the return journey. I had four hours to do it in and it took me ten minutes. After that, I debated whether to go over to the stands and find some lunch, and decided I wasn't hungry. After that, I yawned. It was a habit.

I had been depressed for so long that it had become a permanent state of mind. Expectations might lift the edge of the cloud every time one took a new job, but life never turned out to be as good as the hopes. This was my sixth job since I'd gone to learn flying with stars in my eyes, my fourth since the stars had faded for good. I had thought that taxi flying might be interesting, and after crop spraying, which I'd been doing last, anything would be; and perhaps it would indeed be interesting, but if I'd thought it might be free of gripe and bad temper I'd been kidding myself. For here it all was, as usual. Squabbling passengers and belligerent competitors and no discernible joy anywhere.

There was a small buffet on the side of the fuselage and the jar and sound of someone stepping up onto the wing. The slightly open door was pushed wide with a crash, and into its space appeared a girl, bending at the waist and knees and neck so that she could look inside and across at me.

She was slim and dark-haired and she was wearing large square sunglasses. Also she had on a blue linen dress and long white boots. She looked great. The afternoon instantly improved.

"You lousy bloody skunk," she said.

It really was one of those days.

Chapter Two

"Wow," she said. "Wrong man." She took off the sunglasses and folded them away in the white handbag which hung from her shoulder by a thick red, white, and blue cord.

"Think nothing of it."

"Where's Larry?"

"Gone to Turkey."

"Gone?" she said blankly. "Do you mean literally gone already, or planning to go, or what?"

I looked at my watch. "Took off from Heathrow twenty minutes ago, I believe."

"Damn," she said forcefully. "Bloody damn."

She straightened up so that all I could see of her was from the waist down. A pleasant enough view for any poor aviator. The legs looked about twenty-three years old and there was nothing wrong with them.

She bent down again. Nothing wrong with the rest of her, either.

"When will he be back?"

"He had a three-year contract."

"Oh, *hell.*" She stared at me in dismay for a few seconds, then said, "Can I come in there and talk to you for a minute?"

"Sure," I said, and moved my maps and stuff off Goldenberg's seat. She stepped down into the cockpit and slid expertly into place. By no means her first entrance into a light aircraft. I wondered about Larry. Lucky Larry.

"I suppose he didn't give you . . . a parcel . . . or anything . . . to give me, did he?" she said gloomily.

"Nothing, I'm afraid."

"He's an absolute beast, then. . . . Er, is he a friend of yours?"

"I've met him twice, that's all."

"He's pinched my hundred quid," she said bitterly.

"He's pinched? . . ."

"He bloody has. Not to mention my handbag and keys and everything." She stopped and compressed her mouth in anger. Then she added, "I left my handbag in this airplane three weeks ago, when we flew to Doncaster. And Larry has been saying ever since that he'll bring it on the next trip to the races and give it to Colin to give to me, and for three solid weeks he's kept on forgetting it. I suppose he knew he was going to Turkey, and he thought if he could put it off long enough he would never have to give my bag back."

"Colin . . . Colin Ross?" I asked.

She nodded abstractedly.

"Is he your husband?"

She looked startled, then laughed. "Good Lord, no. He's my brother. I saw him just now in the paddock and I said, 'Has he brought my handbag?' and he shook his head and started to say something, but I belted off over here in a fury without stopping to listen, and I suppose he was going to tell me it wasn't Larry who had come in the plane. . . . Oh, damn it, I *hate* being robbed. Colin would have lent him a hundred quid if he was that desperate. He didn't have to pinch it."

"It was a lot of money to have in a handbag," I suggested.

"Colin had just given it to me, you see. In the plane. Some owner had handed him a terrific present in readies, and he gave me a hundred of it to pay a bill with, which was really sweet of him, and I can hardly expect him to give me another hundred just because I was silly enough to leave the first one lying about. . . ." Her voice trailed off in depression.

16

"The bill," she added wryly, "is for flying lessons."

I looked at her with interest. "How far have you got?"

"Oh, I've got my license," she said. "These were instrument-flying lessons. And radio navigation, and all that jazz. I've done about ninety-five hours, altogether. Spread over about four years, though, sad to say."

That put her in the experienced-beginner class and the dangerous time bracket. After eighty hours' flying, pilots are inclined to think they know enough. After a hundred hours, they are sure they don't. Between the two, the accident rate is at its peak.

She asked me several questions about the airplane, and I answered them. Then she said, "Well, there's no point in sitting here all afternoon," and began to lever herself out onto the wing. "Aren't you coming over to the races?"

"No." I shook my head.

"Oh, come on," she said. "Do."

The sun was shining and she was very pretty. I smiled and said "O.K.," and followed her out onto the grass. It is profitless now to speculate on the different course things would have taken if I'd stayed where I was.

I collected my jacket from the rear baggage compartment and locked all the doors and set off with her across the track. The man on the gate duly let me into the paddock, and Colin Ross's sister showed no sign of abandoning me once we were inside. Instead she diagnosed my almost total ignorance and seemed to be pleased to be able to start dispelling it.

"You see that brown horse over there," she said, steering me toward the parade-ring rails, "That one walking round the far end, Number Sixteen, that's Colin's mount in this race. It's come out a bit light but it looks well in its coat."

"It does?"

She looked at me in amusement. "Definitely."

"Shall I back it, then?"

"It's all a joke to you."

17

"No," I protested.

"Oh, yes, indeed." She nodded. "You're looking at this race meeting in the way I'd look at a lot of spiritualists. Disbelieving and a bit superior."

"Ouch."

"But what you're actually seeing is a large export industry in the process of marketing its wares."

"I'll remember that."

"And if the industry takes place out-of-doors on a nice fine sunny day with everyone enjoying themselves—well, so much the better."

"Put that way," I said, "it's a lot more jolly than a car factory."

"You will get involved," she said with certainty.

"No." I was equally definite.

She shook her head. "You will, you know, if you do much racecourse taxi work. It'll bust through that cool shell of yours and make you feel something, for a change."

I blinked. "Do you always talk like that to total strangers?"

"No," she said slowly, "I don't."

The bright little jockeys flooded into the parade ring and scattered to small earnest owner-trainer groups where there were a lot of serious conversations and much nodding of heads. On the instructions of Colin Ross's sister, I tried moderately hard to take it all seriously. Not with much success.

Colin Ross's sister . . .

"Do you have a name?" I asked.

"Often."

"Thanks."

She laughed. "It's Nancy. What's yours?"

"Matt Shore."

"Hmm. A flat mat name. Very suitable."

The jockeys were thrown up like confetti and landed in their saddles, and their spindly shining long-legged transportation skittered its way out onto the track. Two-year-olds, Nancy said.

She walked me back toward the stands and proposed to smuggle me into the "Owners and Trainers."

The large official at the bottom of the flight of steps beamed at her until his eyes disappeared, and he failed to inspect me for the right bit of cardboard.

It seemed that nearly everyone on the small rooftop stand knew Nancy, and obvious that they agreed with the beaming official's assessment. She introduced me to several people whose interest collapsed like a soufflé in a draft when they found I didn't understand their opening bids.

"He's a pilot," Nancy explained apologetically. "He flew Colin here today."

"Ah," they said. "Ah."

Two of my other passengers were there. Annie Villars was watching the horses canter past with an intent eye and a pursed mouth: the field-marshal element was showing strongly, the feminine camouflage in abeyance. Major Tyderman, planted firmly with his legs apart and his chin tucked well back into his neck, was scribbling notes into his race card. When he looked up, he saw us and made his way purposefully across.

"I say," he said to me, having forgotten my name. "Did I leave my *Sporting Life* over in the plane, do you know?"

"Yes, you did, Major."

"Blast," he said. "I made some notes on it. . . . Must get it, you know. Have to go across after this race."

"Would you like me to fetch it?" I asked.

"Well, that's very good of you, my dear chap. But—no—couldn't ask it. Walk will do me good."

"The aircraft's locked, Major," I said. "You'll need the keys." I took them out of my pocket and gave them to him.

"Right." He nodded stiffly. "Good."

The race started away off down the track and was all over long before I sorted out the colors of Colin Ross. In the event, it wasn't difficult. He had won.

"How's Midge?" Annie Villars said to Nancy, restoring her giant race glasses to their case.

"Oh, much better, thank you. Getting on splendidly."

"I'm so glad. She's had a bad time, poor girl."

19

Nancy nodded and smiled, and everyone trooped down the stairs to the ground.

"Well, now," Nancy said. "How about some coffee? And something to munch, perhaps?"

"You must have others you'd prefer to be with. . . . I won't get into trouble, you know, on my own."

Her lips twitched. "Today I need a bodyguard. I elected you for the job. Desert me if you like, but if you want to please, stick."

"Not difficult," I said.

"Great. Coffee, then."

It was iced coffee, rather good. Halfway through the turkey sandwiches, the reason Nancy wanted me with her drifted up to the small table where we sat and slobbered all over her. She fended off what looked to me like a random assembly of long hair, beard, beads, fringes, and a garment like a tablecloth with a hole in it, and yelled to me through the undergrowth, "Buddy, your job starts right now."

I stood up, reached out two hands, caught hold of an assortment of wool and hair, and pulled firmly backward. The result resolved itself into a surprised youngish man sitting down much more suddenly than he'd intended.

"Nancy," he said in an aggrieved voice.

"This is Chanter," she said to me. "He's never grown out of the hippie thing, as you can see."

"I'm an artist," he said. He had an embroidered band across his forehead and round his head: like the horses' bridles, I thought fleetingly. All the hair was clean, and there were shaven parts on his jaw just to prove that it wasn't from pure laziness that he let everything grow. On closer inspection, I was sure that it was indeed a dark green chenille tablecloth, with a central hole for his head. Underneath that he wore low-slung buckskin trousers fringed from hip to ankle, and a creepy crêpy dim mauve shirt curved to fit his concave stomach. Various necklaces and pendants on silver chains hung round his neck. Under all the splendor he had dirty bare feet.

"I went to art school with him," Nancy said

20

resignedly. "That was in London. Now he's at Liverpool, just down the road. Any time I come racing up here, he turns up, too."

"Uh," Chanter said profoundly.

"Do you get grants forever?" I asked: not sneeringly; I simply wanted to know.

He was not offended. "Look, man, like, up here I'm the fuzz."

I nearly laughed. Nancy said, "You know what he means, then?"

"He teaches," I said.

"Yeah, man, that's what I said." He took one of the turkey sandwiches. His fingers were greenish with black streaks. Paint.

"You keep your impure thoughts off this little bird," he said to me, spitting out bits of bread. "She's strictly my territory. But strictly, man."

"Zat so?"

"Zat definitely—but definitely—is so, man."

"How come?"

He gave me a look which was as offbeat as his appearance.

"I've still got the salt to put on this little bird's tail," he said. "Shan't be satisfied till it's there. . . ."

Nancy was looking at him with an expression which meant that she didn't know whether to laugh at him or be afraid of him. She couldn't decide whether he was Chanter the amorous buffoon or Chanter the frustrated sex maniac. Nor could I. I understood her needing help when he was around.

"He only wants me because I won't," she said.

"The challenge bit." I nodded. "Affront to male pride, and all that."

"Practically every other girl has," she said.

"That makes it worse."

Chanter looked at me broodingly. "You're a drag, man. I mean, cubic."

"To each his scene," I said ironically.

He took the last of the sandwiches, turned his back studiously toward me, and said to Nancy, "Let's you and me lose this dross, huh?"

21

"Let's you and me do nothing of the sort, Chanter. If you want to tag along, Matt comes in the deal."

He scowled at the floor and then suddenly stood up so that all the fringes and beads danced and jingled.

"Come on, then. Let's get a look at the horses. Life's a-wasting."

"He really can draw," Nancy said as we followed the tablecloth out into the sunshine.

"I wouldn't doubt it. I'll bet half of what he does is caricature, though, with a strong element of cruelty."

"How d'you know?" she said, startled.

"He just seems like that."

He padded along beside us in his bare feet and was a sufficiently unusual sight on a racecourse to attract a barrage of stares, ranging from amusement to apoplexy. He didn't seem to notice. Nancy looked as if she were long used to it.

We came to a rest against the parade-ring rails, where Chanter rested his elbows and exercised his voice.

"Horses," he said. "I'm not for the Stubbs and Munnings thing. When I see a racehorse, I see a machine, and that's what I paint, a horse-shaped machine with pistons thumping away and muscle fibers like connecting rods and a crack in the crankcase with the oil dripping away drop by drop into the body cavity—" He broke off abruptly, but with the same breath finished, "How's your sister?"

"She's much better," Nancy said, not seeming to see any great change of subject. "She's really quite well now."

"Good," he said, and went straight on with his lecture. "And then I draw some distant bulging stands with hats flying off and everyone cheering, and all the time the machine is bursting its gut. . . . I see components, I see what's happening to the bits . . . the stresses. . . . I see colors in components, too. . . . Nothing on earth is a whole . . . nothing is ever what it seems . . . everything is components." He stopped abruptly, thinking about what he'd said,

After a suitably appreciative pause, I asked, "Do you ever sell your paintings?"

"Sell them?" He gave me a scornful, superior stare. "No, I don't. Money is disgusting."

"It's more disgusting when you haven't got it," Nancy said.

"You're a renegade, girl," he said fiercely.

"Love on a crust," she said, "is fine when you're twenty, but pretty squalid when you're sixty."

"I don't intend to be sixty. Sixty is strictly for grandfathers. Not my scene at all."

We turned away from the rails and came face to face with Major Tyderman, who was carrying his *Sporting Life* and holding out the aircraft's keys. His gaze swept over Chanter and he controlled himself admirably. Not a twitch.

He handed me the keys, nodded, glanced once more at Chanter, and retreated in good order.

Even for Nancy's sake, the official wouldn't let Chanter up the steps to the "Owners and Trainers." We watched at grass level with Chanter muttering "stinking bourgeois" at regular intervals.

Colin Ross finished second. The crowd booed and tore up a lot of tickets. Nancy looked as though she were long used to that, too.

Between the next two races, we sat on the grass while Chanter gave us the uninterrupted benefit of his views on the evils of money, racism, war, religion, and marriage. It was regulation stuff, nothing new. I didn't say I thought so. During the discourse, he twice without warning stretched over and put his hand on Nancy's breast. Each time, without surprise, she picked it off again by the wrist and threw it back at him. Neither of them seemed to think it needed comment.

After the next race (Colin was third), Chanter remarked that his throat was dry, and Nancy and I obediently followed him off to the Tattersall's bar for lubrication. Coca-Colas for three, splashed out of the bottles by an overworked barmaid. Chanter busily juggled the three glasses so that it was I who paid, which figured.

The bar was only half full but a great deal of space and attention was being taken up by one man, a large tough-looking individual with a penetrating Australian accent. He had an obviously new white plaster cast on his leg and a pair of crutches which he hadn't mastered. His loud laugh rose above the general buzz as he constantly apologized for knocking into people.

"Haven't got the hang of these props yet. . . ."

Chanter regarded him, as he did most things, with some disfavor.

The large Australian went on explaining his state to two receptive acquaintances.

"Mind you, can't say I'm sorry I broke my ankle. Best investment I ever made." The laugh rang out infectiously and most people in the bar began to grin. Not Chanter, of course.

"See, I only paid my premium the week before, and then I fell down these steps and I got a thousand quid for it. Now that ain't whistling, that ain't, eh? A thousand bleeding quid for falling down a flight of steps." He laughed again hugely, enjoying the joke. "Come on, mates," he said, "drink up, and let's go and invest some of this manna from heaven on my good friend Kenny Bayst."

I jumped a fraction and looked at my watch. Coming up to three-thirty. Kenny Bayst clearly hadn't told his good friend not to speculate. Absolutely none of my business. Telling him myself would be the worst favor I could do for Kenny Bayst.

The large Australian swung himself out of the bar, followed by the two mates. Chanter's curiosity overcame his disinclination to show himself at a loss.

"Who," he said crossly, "is going to give that schmo a thousand quid for breaking his ankle?"

Nancy smiled. "It's a new insurance fund, specially for people who go racing. Accident insurance. I don't really know. I've heard one or two people mention it lately."

"Insurance is immoral," Chanter said dogmatically,

24

sliding round behind her and laying his hand flat on her stomach. Nancy picked it off and stepped away. As a bodyguard, I didn't seem to be doing much good.

Nancy said she particularly wanted to see this race properly, and left Chanter looking moody at the bottom of the staircase. Without asking her, I followed her up the steps: a period alone with Chanter held no attractions.

Kenny Bayst, according to my slantwise look at Nancy's race card, was riding a horse called Rudiments: Number 7, owned by the Duke of Wessex, trained by Miss Villars, carrying olive green with silver crossbelts and cap. I watched the horse canter down past the stands on the olive-green grass and reflected that the Duke of Wessex had chosen colors which were as easy to distinguish as coal on a black night.

I said to Nancy, "What did Rudiments do in his last race?"

"Hmm?" she said absent-mindedly, all her attention on the rose-pink-and-white shape of her brother. "Did you say Rudiments?"

"That's right. I brought Kenny Bayst and Annie Villars here, as well."

"Oh. I see." She looked at her race card. "Last time out . . . it won. Time before that, it won. Time before that, it came fourth."

"It's good, then?"

"Fairly, I suppose." She wrinkled her nose at me. "I told you you'd get involved."

I shook my head. "Just curious."

"Same thing."

"Is it favorite?"

"No, Colin is. But—you can see over there, on that big board, see?—Rudiments is second favorite on the Tote at about three to one."

"Well," I said, "what does it mean, to lay a horse?"

"It means to stand a bet. It's what bookmakers do. What the Tote does, really, come to that."

"Can people do it who aren't bookmakers?"

"Oh, sure. They do. Say the bookmakers are offer-

ing three to one, and you yourself don't think the horse
will win, you could say to your friends, I'll lay you
four to one; so they'd bet with you because you were
offering more. Also, no betting tax. Private wager, you
see."

"And if the horse wins, you pay out?"

"You sure do."

"I see," I said. And I did. Eric Goldenberg had laid
Rudiments the last time it had run because Kenny
Bayst had agreed to lose, and then he'd gone and
won. Their tempers were still on the dicky side as a
result; and they had been arguing today about
whether or not to try again.

"Colin thinks he'll win this," Nancy said. "I do hope
so."

Bonanza for Bayst, I thought.

It was a seven-furlong race, it seemed. The horses
accelerated from standing to 30 m.p.h. in times which
would have left a Porsche gasping. When they swung
away round the far bend, Rudiments was as far as I
was concerned invisible, and until the last hundred
yards I didn't see him once. Then all of a sudden
there he was, boxed in in a bunch on the rails and
unable to get past Colin Ross directly in front.

Kenny didn't find his opening. He finished the race
in third place, still pinned in by Colin in front and a
dappled gray alongside. I couldn't begin to tell
whether or not he had done it on purpose.

"Wasn't that *great?*" Nancy exclaimed to the world
in general, and a woman on the far side of her agreed
that it was, and asked after the health of her sister
Midge.

"Oh, she's fine, thanks," Nancy said. She turned to
me, and there was less joy in her eyes than in her
voice. "Come over here," she said. "You can see them
unsaddling the winner."

The "Owners and Trainers" turned out to be on the
roof of the weighing room. We leaned over the rails
at the front and watched Colin and Kenny unbuckle
the saddle girths, loop the saddles over their arms,
pat their steaming horses, and disappear into the

weighing room. The group in the winner's enclosure were busy slapping backs and unburdening to the press. The group in the third enclosure wore small tight smiles and faraway eyes. I still couldn't tell if they were ecstatic and hiding it, or livid and ditto.

The horses were led away and the groups dispersed. In their place appeared Chanter, staring up and waving his arm.

"Come on down!" he shouted.

"No inhibitions, that's his trouble," Nancy said. "If we don't go down, he'll just go on shouting."

He did. An official strode up manfully to ask him to belt up and buzz off, but it was like ripples trying to push over Bass Rock.

"Come on down, Nancy!" Fortissimo.

She pushed herself away from the rails and took enough steps to be out of his sight.

"Stay with me," she said. It was more than half a question.

"If you want it."

"You've seen what he's like. And he's been mild today. Mild. Thanks to you."

"I've done absolutely nothing."

"You're here."

"Why do you come to Haydock, if he always bothers you too much?"

"Because I'm bloody well not letting him frighten me away."

"He loves you," I said.

"No. Can't you tell the difference, for God's sake?"

"Yes," I said.

She looked startled, then shook her head. "He loves Chanter, full stop."

She took three more steps toward the stairs, then stopped again.

"Why is it that I talk to you as if I'd known you for years?"

To a certain extent I knew, but I smiled and shook my head. No one cares to say straight out that it's because one is as negative as wallpaper.

Chanter's plaintive voice floated up the steps. "Nancy, come on down. . . ."

She took another step, and then stopped again. "Will you do me another favor? I'm staying up here a few more days with an aunt, but I bought a present for Midge this morning and I've given it to Colin to take home. But he's got a memory like a string vest for everything except horses, so would you check with him that he hasn't left it in the changing room, before you take off?"

"Sure," I said. "Your sister . . . I gather she's been ill."

She looked away up the sun-filled sky and down again and straight at me, and in a shattering moment of awareness I saw the pain and the cracks behind the bright public façade.

"Has been. Will be," she said. "She's got leukemia."

After a pause, she swallowed and added the unbearable bit.

"She's my identical twin."

Chapter Three

After the fifth race, Chanter gloomily announced that about fifty plastic students were waiting for him to pat their egos and that although he despised the system he was likely to find eating a problem if he actually got the sack. His farewell to Nancy consisted in wiping his hands all over her, front and back, and giving her an openmouthed kiss which, owing to her split-second evasive action, landed on her ear.

He glared at me as if it were my fault. Nancy not relenting, he scowled at her and muttered something about salt, then twirled around on his bare heel, so that the tablecloth and all the hair and fringes and beads swung out with centrifugal force, and strode away at high speed toward the exit.

"The soles of his feet are like leather," she said. "Disgusting." But from the hint of indulgence in her face I gathered that Chanter's cause wasn't entirely lost.

She said she was thirsty again and could do with a Coke, and since she seemed to want me still to tag along, I tagged. This time, without Chanter, we went to the members' bar in the Club enclosure, the small downstairs one that was open to the main entrance hall.

The man in the plaster cast was there again. Different audience. Same story. His big cheerful booming voice filled the little bar and echoed round the whole hall outside.

29

"You can't hear yourself think," Nancy said.

In a huddle in a far corner were Major Tyderman and Eric Goldenberg, sitting at a small table with what looked like treble whiskies in front of them. Their heads were bent toward each other, close, almost touching, so that they could each hear what the other was saying amid the din, yet not be overheard. Relations between them didn't seem to be at their most cordial. There was a great deal of rigidity in their downbent faces, and no friendliness in the small flicking glances they occasionally gave each other.

"The *Sporting Life* man," Nancy said, following my gaze.

"Yes. The big one is a passenger, too."

"They don't look madly happy."

"They weren't madly happy coming up here, either."

"Owners of chronic losers?"

"No—well, I don't think so. They came up because of that horse Rudiments, which Kenny Bayst rode for Annie Villars, but they aren't down in the race card as its owners."

She flicked back through her card. "Rudiments. Duke of Wessex. Well, neither of those two is him, poor old booby."

"Who, the Duke?"

"Yes," she said. "Actually, I suppose he isn't all that old, but he's dreadfully dim. Big important-looking man with a big important-looking rank, and as sweet as they come, really, but there's nothing but cotton wool upstairs."

"You know him well?"

"I've met him often."

"Subtle difference."

"Yes."

The two men scraped back their chairs and began to make their way out of the bar. The man in the plaster cast caught sight of them and his big smile grew even bigger.

"Say, if it isn't Eric—Eric Goldenberg, of all people.

Come over here, me old sport, come and have a drink."

Goldenberg looked less than enthusiastic at the invitation, and the Major sidled away quickly to avoid being included, giving the Australian a glance full of the dislike of the military for the flamboyant.

The man in the cast put one arm clumsily round Goldenberg's shoulder, the crutch swinging out widely and knocking against Nancy.

"Say," he said. "Sorry, lady. I haven't got the hang of these things yet."

"That's all right," she said, and Goldenberg said something to him that I couldn't hear, and before we knew where we were we had been encompassed into the Australian's circle and he was busy ordering drinks all round.

Close to, he was a strange-looking man because his face and hair were almost colorless. The skin was whitish, the scalp, half bald, was fringed by silky hair that had been fair and was turning white, the eyelashes and eyebrows made no contrast, and the lips of the smiling mouth were creamy pale. He looked like a man made up to take the part of a large cheerful ghost. His name, it appeared, was Acey Jones.

"Aw, come on," he said to me in disgust. "Coke is for milksops, not men." Even his eyes were pale: a light indeterminate bluey gray.

"Just lay off him, Ace," Goldenberg said. "He's flying me home. A drunken pilot I can do without."

"A pilot, eh?" The big voice broadcast the information to about fifty people who weren't in the least interested. "One of the flyboys? Most pilots I know are a bunch of proper tearaways. Live hard, love hard, drink hard. Real characters, those guys." He said it with an expansive smile which hid the implied slight. "C'mon now, sport, live dangerously. Don't disillusion all these people."

"Beer, then, please," I said.

Nancy was equally scornful, but for opposite reasons. "Why did you climb down?"

"Antagonizing people when you don't have to is

31

like casting your garbage on the waters. One day it may come floating back, smelling worse."

She laughed. "Chanter would say that was immoral. Stands must be made on principles."

"I won't drink more than half of the beer. Will that do?"

"You're impossible."

Acey Jones handed me the glass and watched me take a mouthful, and went on a bit about hell-raising and beating up the skies and generally living the life of a high-powered gypsy. He made it sound very attractive, and his audience smiled and nodded their heads and none of them seemed to know that the picture was fifty years out of date, and that the best thing a pilot can be is careful: sober, meticulous, receptive, and careful. There are old pilots and foolish pilots, but no old foolish pilots. Me, I was old, young, wise, foolish, thirty-four. Also depressed, divorced, and broke.

After aviation, Acey Jones switched back to insurance and told Goldenberg and Nancy and me and the fifty other people about getting a thousand pounds for breaking his ankle, and we had to listen to it all again, reacting with the best we could do in surprised appreciation.

"No, look—no kidding, sport," he said to Goldenberg, with his first sign of seriousness. "You want to get yourself signed up with this outfit. Best fiver I've ever spent. . . ."

Several of the fifty onlookers edged nearer to listen, and Nancy and I filtered toward the outside of the group. I put down the tasted beer on an inconspicuous table out in the hall while Nancy dispatched the bottom half of her Coke, and from there we drifted out into the air.

The sun was still shining, but the small round white clouds were expanding into bigger round clouds with dark gray centers. I looked at my watch. Four-twenty. Still nearly an hour until the time the Major wanted to leave. The longer we stayed, the bumpier

the ride was likely to be, because the afternoon forecast for scattered thunderstorms looked accurate.

"Cu-nims forming," Nancy said, watching them.
"Nasty."

We went and watched her brother get up on his
mount for the last race, and then we went up on the
"Owners and Trainers" and watched him win it, and
that was about that. She said goodbye to me near the
bottom of the steps, outside the weighing room.

"Thanks for the escort duty. . . ."

"Enjoyed it. . . ."

She had smooth gilded skin and grayish-brown
eyes. Straight dark eyebrows. Not much lipstick. No
scent. Very much the opposite of my blond, painted,
and departed wife.

"I expect," she said, "that we'll meet again, because
I sometimes fly with Colin if there's a spare seat."

"Do you ever take him yourself?"

"Good Lord, no." She laughed. "He wouldn't trust
me to get him there on time. And anyway there are
too many days when the weather is beyond what I can
do. Maybe one day, though. . . ."

She held out her hand and I shook it. A grip very
like her brother's, and just as brief.

"See you, then," she said.

"I hope so."

She nodded with a faint smile and went away. I
watched her neat blue-and-white back view and
stifled a sudden unexpected inclination to run after
her and give her a Chanter-type farewell.

When I walked across the track toward the airplane, I met Kenny Bayst coming back from it with
his raincoat over his arm. His skin was blotched pink
again with fury, clashing with his carroty hair.

"I'm not coming back with you," he said tightly.
"You tell Miss Annie effing Villars that I'm not coming back with you. There's no bloody pleasing her.
Last time I nearly got the push for winning, and this
time I nearly got the push for not winning. You'd

think that both times I'd had the slightest choice in the matter. I'll tell you straight, sport, I'm not coming back in your bloody little airplane having them gripe, gripe, gripe at me all the way back."

"All right," I said. I didn't blame him.

"I've just been over to fetch my raincoat. I'll go home by train—or get a lift."

"Raincoat . . . but the aircraft is locked."

"No, it isn't. I just got my raincoat out of the back. Now, you tell them I've had enough, right?"

I nodded, and while he hurried off I walked on toward the airplane, a bit annoyed. Major Tyderman should have locked up again after he had fetched his *Sporting Life,* but apparently he hadn't.

Both the doors on the port side were unlocked, the passenger door and the baggage locker. I wasn't too pleased, because Derrydowns had told me explicitly never to leave the aircraft open, as they'd had damage done by small boys on several occasions: but all looked well and there were no signs of sticky fingers.

I did the external checks again and glanced over the flight plan for the return. If we had to avoid too many thunderclouds, it might take a little longer to reach Newmarket, but unless there was one settled and active over the landing field there should be no problem.

The passengers of the two Polyplane aircraft assembled by ones and twos, shoveled themselves inside, shut the doors, and were trundled down to the far end of the course. One after the other, the two airplanes raced back over the grass and lifted away, wheeling like black darts against the blue, gray, and white patchwork of the sky.

Annie Villars came first of my lot. Alone, composed, polite; giving nothing away. She handed me her coat and binoculars and I stored them for her. She thanked me. The deceptive mild brown eyes held a certain blankness, and every few seconds a spasmodic tightening belied the gentle set of her mouth. A formidable lady, I thought. What was more, she herself knew it. She was so conscious of the strength and

range of her power that she deliberately manufac-
tured the disarming exterior in order not exactly to
hide it, but to make it palatable. Made a nice change,
I thought ironically, from all those who put up a big
tough front to disguise their inner lack.

"Kenny Bayst asked me to tell you that he has got a
lift home to Newmarket and won't be coming back
by air," I said.

A tiny flash of fire in the brown eyes. The gentle
voice, completely controlled, said, "I'm not surprised."
She climbed into the airplane and strapped herself
into her seat and sat there in silence, looking out over
the emptying racecourse with eyes that weren't concentrating on the grass and the trees.

Tyderman and Goldenberg returned together, still
deep in discussion. The Major's side mostly consisted
of decisive nods, but words were pouring out of Goldenberg. Also he was past worrying about what I overheard.

"I would be surprised if the little shit hasn't been
double-crossing us all the time and collecting from
some bookmaker or other even more than he got from
us. Making fools of us, that's what he's been doing. I'll
murder the little sod. I told him so, too."

"What did he say?" the Major asked.

"Said I wouldn't get the chance. Cocky little
bastard."

They thrust their gear angrily into the baggage
compartment and stood talking by the rear door in
voices rumbling like the distant thunder.

Colin Ross came last, slight and inconspicuous, still
wearing the faded jeans and the now crumpled sweat
shirt.

I went a few steps to meet him. "Your sister Nancy
asked me to check with you whether you had remembered to bring the present for Midge."

"Oh, damn. . . ." More than irritation in his voice,
there was weariness. He had ridden six hard races,
won three of them. He looked as if a toddler could
knock him down.

"I'll get it for you, if you like."

35

"Would you?" He hesitated, then with a tired flap of his wrist said, "Well, I'd be grateful. Go into the weighing room and ask for my valet, Ginger Mundy. The parcel's on the shelf over my peg. He'll get it for you."

I nodded and went back across the track. The parcel, easily found, proved to be a little smaller than a shoe box and was wrapped in pink-and-gold paper with a pink ribbon bow. I took it over to the airplane, and Colin put it on Kenny Bayst's empty seat.

The Major had already strapped himself in and was drumming with his fingers on his binocular case, which was as usual slung around him. His body was still stiff with tension. I wondered if he ever relaxed.

Goldenberg waited without a smile while I clambered across into my seat, then followed me in and clipped shut the door in gloomy silence. I sighed, started the engine, and taxied down to the far end of the course. Ready for takeoff, I turned round to my passengers and tried a bright smile.

"All set?"

I got three grudging nods for my pains. Colin Ross was asleep. I took the hilarious party off the ground without enthusiasm, skirted the Manchester zone, and pointed the nose in the general direction of Newmarket. Once up in the sky, it was all too clear that the air had become highly unstable. At lower levels, rising pockets of heat from the built-up areas bumped the airplane about like a puppet, and to enormous heights great heaps of cumulo-nimbus cloud were boiling up all round the horizon.

Airsick-making weather. I looked round to see if an issue of water-proof bags was going to be required. Needn't have bothered. Colin was still asleep, and the other three had too much on their minds to worry about a few lurches. I told Annie Villars where the bags were to be found if wanted, and she seemed to think I had insulted her.

Although by four thousand feet the worst of the bumps were below us, the flight was a bit like a bending race as I tracked left and right to avoid the dark towering cloud masses. Mostly we stayed in the sunshine: occasionally raced through the small veiling clouds which were dotted among the big ones. I wanted to avoid even the medium-sized harmless ones, as these sometimes hid a dangerous whopper just behind, and at 150 m.p.h. there was little chance to dodge. Inside every well-grown cumulo-nimbus, there were vertical rushing air currents which could lift and drop even an airliner like a yo-yo. Also one could meet hailstones and freezing rain. Nobody's idea of a jolly playground. So it was a good idea to avoid the black churning brutes, but it was a rougher ride than one should aim for with passengers.

Everyone knows the horrible skin-prickling heart-thudding feeling when the normal suddenly goes wrong. Fear, it's called. The best place to feel it is not with a jerk at four thousand feet in a battlefield of cu-nims.

I was used to far worse weather; to bad, beastly, even lethal weather. It wasn't the state of the sky which distracted me, which set the fierce little adrenalin-packed alarm bell ringing like crazy.

There was something wrong with the airplane.

Nothing much. I couldn't even tell what it was. But something. Something . . .

My instinct for safety was highly developed. Over-developed, many had said when it had got me into trouble. Bloody coward was how they'd put it.

You couldn't ignore it, though. When the instinct switched to danger, you couldn't risk ignoring it, not with passengers on board. What you could do when you were alone was a different matter, but civil commercial pilots seldom got a chance to fly alone.

Nothing wrong with the instruments. Nothing wrong with the engine.

Something wrong with the flying controls.

When I swerved gently to avoid yet another lurking cu-nim, the nose of the aircraft dropped and I had a shade of difficulty pulling it up again. Once level, nothing seemed wrong. All the gauges seemed

37

right. Only the instinct remained. Instinct and the
memory of a slightly sluggish response.

The next time I made a turn, the same thing happened. The nose wanted to drop, and it needed more
pressure than it should have done to hold it level. At
the third turn, it was worse.

I looked down at the map on my knees. We were
twenty minutes out of Haydock . . . south of Matlock
. . . approaching Nottingham. Another eighty nautical
miles to Newmarket.

It was the hinged part of the tail plane which
raised or lowered the aircraft's nose. The elevators,
they were called. They were linked by wires to the
control column in such a way that when you pushed
the control column forward the tail went up and
tipped the nose down. And vice versa.

The wires ran through rings and over pulleys, between the cabin floor and the outer skin of the fuselage. There wasn't supposed to be any friction.

Friction was what I could feel.

I thought perhaps one of the wires had somehow
come off one of the pulleys during the bumpy ride.
I'd never heard of it happening before, but that didn't
mean it couldn't. Or perhaps a whole pulley had come
adrift, or had broken in half. . . . If something was rolling around loose, it could affect the controls fairly
seriously.

I turned to the cheerful company.

"I'm very sorry, but there will be a short delay on
the journey. We're going to land for a while at the
East Midlands Airport, near Nottingham, while I get
a quick precautionary check done on the aircraft."

I met opposition.

Goldenberg said belligerently, "I can't see anything
wrong." His eyes swept over the gauges, noticing all
the needles pointing to the green safety segments on
all the engine instruments. "It all looks the same as it
always does."

"Are you sure it's necessary?" Annie Villars said. "I
particularly want to get back to see my horses at
evening stables."

The Major said "Damn it all!" fiercely and frowned heavily and looked more tense than ever.

They woke up Colin Ross.

"The pilot wants to land here and make what he calls a precautionary check. We want to go straight on. We don't want to waste time. There isn't anything wrong with the plane, as far as we can see. . . ."

Colin Ross's voice came across, clear and decisive. "If he says we're going down, we're going down. He's the boss."

I looked round at them. Except for Colin, they were all more moody and gloomy than ever. Colin unexpectedly gave me a flicker of a wink. I grinned as much to myself as to him, called up East Midlands on the radio, announced our intention to land, and asked them to arrange for a mechanic to be available for a check.

On the way down, I regretted it. The friction seemed no worse: if anything, it was better. Even in the turbulent air near the ground, I had no great trouble in moving the elevators. I'd made a fool of myself and the passengers would be furious and Derrydowns would be scathing about the unnecessary expense, and at any time at all I would be looking for my seventh job.

It was a normal landing. I parked where directed on the apron and suggested everyone get out and go into the airport for a drink, as the check would take half an hour, and maybe more.

They were by then increasingly annoyed. Up in the air, they must have had a lingering doubt that I was right about landing. Safe on the ground, they were becoming sure it was unnecessary.

I walked some of the way across the tarmac with them toward the airport passenger doors, then peeled off to go to the control office for the routine report after landing, and to ask for the mechanic to come for a look-see as soon as possible. I would fetch them from the bar, I said, once the check was done.

"Hurry it up," Goldenberg said rudely.

"Most annoying. Most annoying indeed." The Major.

"I was away last night. ... Particularly wanted to get back early this evening. Might as well go by road, no point in paying for speed if you don't get it." Annie Villars' irritation overcoming the velvet glove.

Colin Ross said, "If your horse coughs, don't race it."

The others looked at him sharply. I said "Thanks" gratefully, and bore off at a tangent to the left. I saw them out of the side of my vision, looking briefly back toward the aircraft and then walking unenthusiastically toward the big glass doors.

There was a crack behind me like a snapping branch, and a monstrous boom, and a roaring gust of air.

I'd heard that sequence before. I spun round, appalled.

Where there had stood a smart little blue-and-white Cherokee there was an exploding ball of fire.

Chapter Four

The bomb had taken a fraction of a second to detonate. The public impact lasted three days. The investigations dragged on for weeks.

Predictably, the dailies went to town on "COLIN ROSS ESCAPES DEATH BY ONE MINUTE" and "CHAMPION JOCKEY WINS RACE AGAINST TIME." Annie Villars, looking particularly sweet and frail, said in a television news interview that we had all been fantastically lucky. Major Tyderman was quoted as saying, "Fortunately there was something wrong with the plane, and we landed for a check. Otherwise . . ." And Colin Ross had apparently finished his sentence for him: "Otherwise we would all have been raining down on Nottingham in little bits."

That was after they had recovered, of course. When I reached them at a run near the airport doors, their eyes were stretched wide and their faces were stiff with shock. Annie Villars' mouth had dropped open and she was shaking from head to foot. I put my hand on her arm. She looked at me blankly and then made a small mewing sound and crumpled against me in a thoroughly un-Napoleonic faint. I caught her on the way down and lifted her up in my arms to save her falling on the shower-soaked tarmac. She weighed even less than she looked.

"God," said Goldenberg automatically. "God." His mind and tongue seemed to be stuck on the single word.

41

The Major's mouth was trembling and he was losing the battle to keep it still with his teeth. Sweat stood out in fine drops on his forehead and he was breathing in short shocked gasps.

Holding Annie Villars, I stood beside them and watched the death throes of the airplane. The first explosion had blown it apart, and almost immediately the fuel tanks had ignited and finished the job. The wreckage lay strewn in burning twisted pieces over a radius of wet tarmac, the parts looking too small ever to have formed the whole. Rivers of burning petrol ran among them, and great curling orange-and-yellow flames roared round the largest piece, which looked like the front part of the cabin.

My seat. My hot, hot seat.

Trouble followed me around like the rats of Hamelin.

Colin Ross looked as shocked as the others, but his nerves were of sterner stuff. "Was that . . . a bomb?"

"Nothing but," I said flippantly.

He looked at me sharply. "It's not funny."

"It's not tragic, either," I said. "We're still here."

A lot of the stiffness left his face and body. The beginnings of a smile appeared. "So we are," he said.

Someone in the control tower had pressed the panic button. Fire engines screamed up, and foam poured out of the giant hoses onto the pathetic scraps. The equipment was designed to deal with jumbos. It took about ten seconds to reduce the Cherokee-sized flames to black memories.

Three or four airport cars buzzed around like gnats, and one filled with agitated officials dashed in our direction.

"Are you the people who came in that aircraft?"

The first of the questions. By no means the last. I knew what I was in for. I had been taken apart before.

"Which is the pilot? Will you come with us, then, and your passengers can go to the manager's office. . . . Is the lady injured?"

"Fainted," I said.

"Oh ..." He hesitated. "Can someone else take her?" He looked at the others. Goldenberg, large and flabby; the Major, elderly; Colin, frail. His eyes passed over Colin and then went back, widening, the incredulity fighting against recognition.

"Excuse me ... are you?"

"Ross," said Colin flatly. "Yes."

They rolled out the red carpet, after that. They produced smelling salts and a ground hostess for Annie Villars, stiff brandies for the Major and Goldenberg, autograph books for Colin Ross. The manager himself took charge of them. And someone excitedly rang up the national press.

The Board of Trade investigators were friendly and polite. As usual. And persistent, scrupulous, and ruthless. As usual.

"Why did you land at East Midland?"

Friction.

"Had you any idea there was a bomb on board?"

No.

"Had you made a thorough preflight investigation?"

Yes.

"And no bomb?"

No.

Did I know that I was nevertheless responsible for the safety of the aircraft and could technically be held responsible for having initiated a flight with a bomb on board?

Yes.

We looked at each other. It was an odd rule. Very few people who took off with a bomb on board lived to be held responsible. The Board of Trade smiled, to show they knew it was silly to think anyone would take off with a bomb, knowing it was there.

"Did you lock the aircraft whenever you left it?"

I did.

"And did it remain locked?"

The knife was in. I told them about the Major. They already knew.

43

"He says he is sure that he relocked the doors," they said. "But even so wasn't it your responsibility to look after the safety of the aircraft, not his?"

Quite so.

"Wouldn't it have been prudent of you to accompany him to fetch the paper?"

No comment.

"The safety of the aircraft is the responsibility of the captain."

Whichever way you turned, it came back to that.

This was my second interview with the Board of Trade. The first, the day after the explosion, had been friendly and sympathetic, a fact-finding mission during which the word "responsibility" had not cropped up once. It had hovered delicately in the wings. Inevitably it would be brought on later and pinned to someone's chest.

"During the past three days, we have interviewed all your passengers, and none of them has any idea who would have wanted to kill them, or why. We now feel we must go more carefully into the matter of opportunity, so we do hope you won't mind answering what may be a lot of questions. Then we can piece together a statement for you, and we would be glad if you would sign it. . . ."

"Do all I can," I said. Dig my own grave. Again.

"They all agreed that the bomb must have been in the gift-wrapped parcel which you yourself carried on board."

Nice.

"And that the intended victim was Colin Ross."

I sucked my teeth.

"You don't think so?"

"I honestly have no idea who it was intended for," I said. "But I don't think the bomb was in the parcel."

"Why not?"

"His sister bought it, that morning."

"We know." He was a tall man, with inward-looking eyes, as if they were consulting a computer in his head, feeding in every answer he was given, and waiting for the circuits to click out a conclusion.

There was no aggression anywhere in his manner, no vengeance in his motivation. A fact finder, a cause seeker: like a truffle hound. He knew the scent of truth. Nothing would entice him away.

"And it sat on a shelf in the changing room all afternoon," I said. "And no one is allowed into the changing room except jockeys and valets."

"We understand that that is so." He smiled. "Could the parcel have been the bomb? Weightwise?"

"I suppose so."

"Miss Nancy Ross says it contained a large fancy bottle of bath oil."

"No pieces in the wreckage?" I asked.

"Not a thing." The tall man's nose wrinkled. "I've seldom seen a more thorough disintegration."

We were sitting in what was called the crew room in the Derrydowns office on the old R.A.F. airfield near Buckingham. Such money as Derrydowns spent on appearances began in the manager's office and ended in the passengers' waiting lounge across the hall. The crew room looked as if the paint and the walls were coming up to their silver wedding. The linoleum had long passed the age of consent. Three of the four cheap armchairs looked as if they had still to reach puberty, but the springs in the fourth were so badly broken that it was more comfortable to sit on the floor.

Much of the wall space was taken up by maps and weather charts and various "Notices to Airmen," several of them out of date. There was a duty roster upon which my name appeared with the utmost regularity, and a notice typed in red capitals to the effect that anyone who failed to take the aircraft's documents with him on a charter flight would get the sack. I had duly taken all the Cherokee's records and maintenance certificates with me, as the Air Navigation Order insisted. Now they were burned to a crisp. I hoped someone somewhere saw some sense in it.

The tall man looked carefully round the dingy room. The other—shorter, broader, silent—sat with his green bitten HB poised over his spiral-bound notebook.

45

"Mr. Shore, I understand you hold an airline transport pilot's license. And a flight navigator's certificate."

He had been looking me up. I knew he would have.

I said flatly, "Yes."

"This taxi work is hardly—well, what you were intended for."

I shrugged.

"The highest possible qualifications. . . ." He shook his head. "You were trained by B.O.A.C. and flew for them for nine years. First officer. In line for captain. And then you left."

"Yes." And they never took you back. Policy decision. Never.

He delicately consulted his notes. "And then you flew as captain for a private British airline until it went into liquidation? And after that for a South American airline, who, I believe, dismissed you. And then all last year a spot of gunrunning, and this spring some crop spraying. And now this."

They never let go. I wondered who had compiled the list.

"It wasn't guns. Food and medical supplies in, refugees and wounded out."

He smiled faintly. "To some remote African airstrip on dark nights? Being shot at?"

I looked at him.

He spread out his hands, "Yes. I know. All legal and respectable, and not our business, of course." He cleared his throat. "Weren't you the—er—the subject—of an investigation about four years ago? While you were flying for British Interport?"

I took in a slow breath. "Yes."

"Mmm." He looked up, down, and sideways. "I've read an outline of that case. They didn't suspend your license."

"No."

"Though, on the face of it, one might have expected them to."

I didn't answer.

"Did Interport pay the fine for you?"

"No."

"But they kept you on as captain. You were convicted of gross negligence, but they kept you on." It was halfway between a statement and a question.

"That's right," I said.

If he wanted all the details, he could read the full report. He knew it and I knew it. He wasn't going to get me to tell him.

He said, "Yes. . . . Well. Who put this bomb in the Cherokee? When and how?"

"I wish I knew."

His manner hadn't changed. His voice was still friendly. We both ignored his tentative shot at piling on the pressure.

"You stopped at White Waltham and Newbury. . . ."

"I didn't lock up at White Waltham. I parked on the grass outside the reception lounge. I could see the airplane most of the time, and it was only on the ground for half an hour. I got there early. . . . I can't see that anyone had a chance, or could rely on having a chance, to put a bomb on board at White Waltham."

"Newbury?"

"They all stayed in their seats except me. Colin Ross came. . . . We put his overnight bag in the front baggage locker. . . ."

The tall man shook his head. "The explosion was further back. Behind the captain's seat, at the very least. The blast evidence makes it certain. Some of the metal parts of the captain's seat were embedded in the instrument panel."

"One minute," I said reflectively. "Very nasty."

"Yes. . . . Who had an opportunity at Haydock?"

I sighed inwardly. "I suppose anyone, from the time I gave the keys to Major Tyderman until I went back to the aircraft."

"How long was that?"

I'd worked it out. "Getting on for three hours. But . . ."

"But what?"

"No one could have counted on the aircraft being
left unlocked."

"Trying to wriggle out?"

"Do you think so?"

He dodged an answer, said: "I'll give it to you that
no one could have known whether it would be locked
or unlocked. You just made it easy."

"All right," I said. "If you'll also bear in mind that
pickers and stealers unlock locked cars every day of
the week, and that aircraft keys are the same type.
Anyone who could manufacture and plant a bomb
could open a little old lock."

"Possibly," he said, and repeated, "But you made it
easy."

Damn Major Tyderman, I thought bleakly. Stupid,
careless old fool. I stifled the thought that I probably
would have gone across with him, or insisted on
fetching his newspaper for him, if I hadn't been un-
willing to walk away and leave Nancy.

"Who could have had access ... leaving aside the
matter of locks?"

I shrugged one shoulder. "All the world. They had
only to walk across the track."

"The aircraft was parked opposite the stands, I
believe, in full view of the crowds."

"Yes. About a hundred yards, in fact, from the
stands. Not close enough for anyone to see exactly
what someone was doing, if he seemed to be walking
round peering in through the windows. People do
that, you know, pretty often."

"You didn't notice anyone yourself?"

I shook my head. "I looked across several times
during the afternoon. Just a casual glance, though. I
wasn't thinking about trouble."

"Hmm." He reflected for a few seconds. Then he
said, "Two of the Polyplanes were there as well, I
believe."

"Yes."

"I think I'd better talk to the pilots, to see if they
noticed anything."

48

I didn't comment. His eyes suddenly focused on mine, sharp and black.

"Were they friendly?"

"The pilots? Not particularly."

"How's the feud?"

"What feud?"

He stared at me assessingly. "You're not that dumb. No one could work for Derrydowns and not know that they and Polyplanes are permanently engaged in scratching each other's eyes out."

I sighed. "I don't give a damn."

"You will when they start reporting you."

"Reporting me? For what? What do you mean?"

He smiled thinly. "If you infringe the rules by as much as one foot, Polyplanes will be on to us before your wheels have stopped rolling. They're doing their best to put Derrydowns out of business. Most of it we shrug off as simply spite. But if they catch you breaking the regulations, and can produce witnesses, we'd have to take action."

"Charming."

He nodded. "Aviation will never need a special police force to detect crime. Everyone is so busy informing on everyone else. Makes us laugh, sometimes."

"Or cry," I said.

"That, too." He nodded wryly. "There are no permanent friendships in aviation. The people you think are your friends are the first to deny they associate with you at the faintest hint of trouble. The cock crows until it's hoarse, in aviation." The bitterness in his voice was unmistakable. But impersonal, also.

"You don't approve."

"No. It makes our job easier, of course. But I like less and less the sight of people scrambling to save themselves at any cost to others. It diminishes them. They are small."

"You can't always blame them for not always wanting to be involved. Aviation law cases are so fierce, so unforgiving. . . ."

49

"Did your friends at Interport rally round and cheer you up?"

I thought back to those weeks of loneliness. "They waited to see."

He nodded. "Didn't want to be contaminated."

"It's a long time ago," I said.

"You never forget rejection," he said. "It's a trauma."

"Interport didn't reject me. They kept me on for another year, until they went bust. And," I added, "I didn't have anything to do with *that*."

He gently laughed. "Oh, I know. My masters the Government put on one of its great big squeezes, and by one means or another forced them out of business."

I didn't pursue it. The history of aviation was littered with the bodies of murdered air firms. Insolvency sat like a vulture in every board room in the industry and constantly pecked away at the bodies before they were dead. British Eagle, Handley Page, Beagle—the list of corpses was endless. Interport had been one of the largest, and Derrydowns, still struggling, one of the smallest, but their problems were identical. Huge inexorable costs. Fickle variable income. Write the sum in red.

I said, "There is one other place, of course, where the bomb could have been put on board." I stopped.

"Spell it out, then."

"Here."

The tall investigator and his silent friend with the pencil went down to the hangar to interview old Joe.

Harley called me into his office.

"Have they finished?"

"They've gone to ask Joe if he put the bomb in the Cherokee."

Harley was irritated, which was with him a common state of mind. "Ridiculous."

"Or if Larry did."

"*Larry* . . ."

"He left for Turkey that afternoon," I pointed out. "Would he have planted a legacy?"

50

"No." Short, snappy, and vehement.

"Why did he leave?"

"He wanted to." He gave me a sharp glance bordering on dislike. "You sound like the Board of Trade."

"Sorry," I said in conciliation. "Must be catching."

Harley's office dated back to a more prosperous past. There was a carpet of sorts on the floor and the walls had been painted within living memory, and his good-quality desk had mellowed instead of chipping. Limp blue curtains framed the big window looking out over the airfield and several good photographs of airplanes had been framed and hung. Customers, when they visited him, were allowed the nearly new lightweight armchair; crew sat on the wooden upright.

Harley himself was proprietor, manager, chief flying instructor, booking clerk, and window cleaner. His staff consisted of one qualified mechanic past retiring age, one part-time boy helper, one full-time taxi pilot (me), and one part-time pilot who switched from taxiing to teaching, whichever was required, and on alternate days taught in a flying club twenty miles to the north.

Derrydowns' other assets had been, before the Cherokee blew up, three useful aircraft and one bright girl.

The remaining two aircraft were a small single-engine trainer and a twin-engine eight-year-old Aztec, equipped with every possible flying aid, for which Harley was paying through the nose on a five-year lease.

The girl, Honey, his brother's daughter, worked for love and peanuts and was the keystone which held up the arch. I knew her voice better than her face, as she sat up in the control tower all day directing such air traffic as came along. Betweentimes she typed all the letters, kept the records, did the accounts, answered the telephone if her uncle didn't, and collected landing fees from visiting pilots. She was reputed to be suffering from a broken heart about Larry and consequently came down from her crow's nest as seldom as possible.

"She's made puffballs out of her eyes, crying for that louse" was how my part-time colleague put it. "But you wait just a week or two. She'll lie down for you instead. Never refused a good pilot yet, our Honey hasn't."

"How about you?" I asked, amused.

"Me? She'd squeezed me like a lemon long before that Goddamned Larry ever turned up."

Harley said crossly, "We've lost two charters since the bomb. They say the Aztec's too expensive; they would rather go by road." He ran his hand over his head. "There's another Cherokee Six up at Liverpool that's available to lease. I've just been talking to them on the phone. It sounds all right. They're bringing it across here tomorrow afternoon, so you can take it up when you get back from Newmarket and see what you think."

"How about the insurance on the old one?" I asked idly. "It would be cheaper in the long run to buy rather than lease."

"It was on hire-purchase," he said gloomily. "We'll be lucky if we get a penny. And it's not really your business."

Harley was slightly plump and slightly bald and just not quite forceful enough to lift Derrydowns up by its bootstraps. His manner to me was more bossy than friendly, a reaction I understood well enough.

"The last person on earth to put a bomb on any aircraft would be Joe," he said explosively. "He looks after them like a mother. He *polishes* them."

It was true. The Derrydowns aircraft sparkled outside and were shampooed inside. The engines ran like silk. The general slightly misleading air of prosperity which clung around the public face of the firm was mostly Joe's work.

The Board of Trade came back from the hanger looking vaguely sheepish. The rough side of Joe's tongue, I guessed. At sixty-nine and with savings in the bank, he was apt to lay down his own laws. He had taken exception to my theory that a pulley on the elevator wires had come adrift. No such thing was possible in one of his aircraft, he had told me stiffly, and I could take my four gold rings away and I knew what I could do with them. As I hadn't worn my captain's jacket for nearly two years, I told him the moths had beaten me to it, and although it was a feeble joke he gave me a less sour look and told me it couldn't have been a broken pulley, he was sure it couldn't, and if it was, it was the manufacturer's fault, not his.

"It saved Colin Ross's life," I pointed out. "You should be claiming a medal for it." Which opened his mouth and shut him up.

The Board of Trade trooped into Harley's office. The tall man sat in the armchair and Green Pencil on the hard one. Harley behind his desk. I leaned against the wall, on my feet.

"Well, now," said the tall man. "It seems as if everyone on this airfield had a chance to tamper with the Cherokee. Everyone in the company, and any customers who happened to be here that morning, and any member of the public wandering around for a look-see. We've assumed the bomb was aimed at Colin Ross, but we don't really know that. If it was, someone had a pretty accurate idea of when he would be in the aircraft."

"Last race four-thirty. He was riding in it," Harley said. "Doesn't take too much figuring to assume that at five-forty he'd be in the air."

"Five-forty-seven," said the tall man. "Actually."

"Any time about then," said Harley irritably.

"I wonder what the bomb was *in*," said the tall man reflectively. "Did you look inside the first-aid tin?"

"No," I said, startled. "I just checked that it was there. I've never looked inside it. Or inside the fire extinguishers, or under the seats or inside the life-jacket covers. . . ."

The tall man nodded. "It could have been in any of those places. Or it could, after all, have been in that fancy parcel."

"Ticking away," said Harley.

I peeled myself slowly off the wall. "Suppose," I

53

said hesitantly, "suppose it wasn't in any of those places. Suppose it was deeper, out of sight. Somewhere between the cabin wall and the outside skin—like a limpet mine, for instance. Suppose that that bumpy ride—and all those turns I did to avoid the cu-nims—dislodged it, so that it was getting jammed in the elevator wires. . . . Suppose that was what I could feel—and why I decided to land—and that what saved us was the bomb itself."

Chapter Five

The next day, I took five jockeys and trainers from Newmarket to Newcastle races and back in the Aztec, and listened to them grousing over the extra expense, and in the evening I tried out the replacement Cherokee, which flew permanently left wing down on the autopilot, had an unserviceable fuel-flow meter, and had an overload somewhere on the electrical circuit.

"It isn't very good," I told Harley. "It's old and noisy and it probably drinks fuel and I shouldn't think the battery's charging properly."

He interrupted me. "It flies. And it's cheap. And Joe will fix it. I'm taking it."

"Also it's orange and white, just like the Polyplanes."

He gave me an irritable glare. "I'm not blind. I know it is. And it's not surprising, considering it used to belong to them."

He waited for me to protest so that he could slap me down, so I didn't. I shrugged instead. If he wanted to admit to his bitterest rivals that his standards were down to one of their third-hand clapped-out old buggies, that was his business.

He signed the lease on the spot and gave it to the pilot who had brought the airplane to take back with him on the train, and the pilot smiled a pitying smile and went off shaking his head.

The orange-and-white Cherokee went down to the

hangar for Joe to wave his wand over, and I walked round the perimeter track to home sweet home.

One caravan, pilots', for the use of. Larry had lived in it before me, and others before him: Harley's taxi pilots stayed, on average, eight months, and most of them settled for the caravan because it was easiest. It stood on a dusty square of concrete which had once been the floor of an R.A.F. hut, and it was connected to the electricity, water, and drainage mains which had served the long-departed airmen.

As caravans go, it must once have held up its head, but generations of beer-drinking bachelors had left tiny teeth marks of bottle caps along the edges of all the fitments, and circular greasy head marks on the wall above every seat. Airport dirt had clogged the brown haircord upholstery into a grayish cake, relieved here and there by darker irregular stains. Shabby pin-ups of superhuman mammalian development were stuck to the walls with tape, and a scatter of torn-off patches of paint showed where dozens of others had been stuck before. Tired green curtains had opened and shut on a thousand hangovers. The flyblown mirror had stared back at a lot of disillusion, and the bedsprings sagged from the weight of a bored succession of pilots with nothing to do except Honey.

I had forgotten to get anything to eat. There was half a packet of cornflakes in the kitchen and a jar of instant coffee. Neither was much use, as yesterday's half pint of milk had gone sour in the heat. I damned it all and slouched on the two-seat approximation to a sofa, and resignedly dragged out of my pocket the two letters which had lain unopened there since that morning.

One was from a television rental firm who said they confirmed that they were transferring the rental from Larry's name to mine, as requested, and could I now be so good as to pay immediately the six weeks for which he was in arrears. The other, from Susan, said briefly that I was late with the alimony yet again.

I put down both the letters and stared unseeingly through the opposite window toward the darkening summer sky. All the empty airfield stretched away into the dusk, calm, quiet, undemanding, and shadowy—everything I needed for a few repairs to the spirit. The only trouble was the process was taking longer than I'd expected. I wondered sometimes whether I'd ever get back to where I'd once been. Maybe if you'd hashed up your life as thoroughly as I had, there was never any going back. Maybe one day soon I'd stop wanting to. Maybe one day I would accept the unsatisfactory present not as a healing period but as all there was ever going to be. That would be a pity, I thought. A pity to let the void take over for always.

I had three pounds in my pocket and sixteen in the bank, but I had finally paid all my debts. The crippling fine, the divorce, and the mountainous bills Susan had run up everywhere in a cold orgy of hatred toward me in the last weeks we were together—everything had been settled. The house had always been in her name because of the nature of my job, and she had clung to that like a leech. She was still living in it, triumphant, collecting a quarter of everything I earned and writing sharp little letters if I didn't pay on the nail.

I didn't understand how love could curdle so abysmally: looking back, I still couldn't understand. We had screamed at each other: hit each other, intending to hurt. Yet when we married, at nineteen, we'd been entwined in tenderness, inseparable and sunny. When it started to go wrong, she said it was because I was away so much, long ten-day tours to the West Indies all the time, and all she had was her job as a doctor's secretary and the dull endless housework. In an uprush of affection and concern for her, I resigned from B.O.A.C. and joined Interport instead, where I flew short-haul trips, and spent most of my nights at home. The pay was a shade less good, the prospects a lot less good, but for about three months we were happier. After that, there was a long period in which

57

we both tried to make the best of it, and a last six months in which we had torn each other's nerves and emotions to shreds.

Since then, I had tried more or less deliberately not to feel anything for anybody. Not to get involved. To be private, and apart, and cold. An ice pack after the tempest.

I hadn't done anything to improve the caravan, to stamp anything of myself upon it. I didn't suppose I would, because I didn't feel the need. I didn't want to get involved, not even with a caravan.

And certainly not with Tyderman, Goldenberg, Annie Villars, and Colin Ross.

All of them except Goldenberg were on my next racing trip.

I had spent two more days in the Aztec, chauffeuring some business executives on their regular monthly visit to subsidiary factories in Germany and Luxembourg, but by Saturday Joe had tarted up the replacement Cherokee, so I set off in that. The fuel-flow meter still resolutely pointed to naught, which was slightly optimistic, but the electrical fault had been cured: no overload now on the generator. And if it still flew one wing low, at least the wing in question sparkled with a new shine. The cabin smelt of soap and air freshener, and all the ashtrays were empty.

The passengers were to be collected that day at Cambridge, and although I flew into the airport half an hour early, the Major was already there, waiting on a seat in a corner of the entrance hall.

I saw him before he saw me, and as I walked toward him he took the binoculars out of their case and put them on the low table beside him. The binoculars were smaller than the case suggested. In went his hand again and out came a silver-and-pigskin flask. The Major took a six-second swig and, with a visible sigh, screwed the cap back into place.

I slowed down and let him get the binoculars back on top of his courage before I came to a halt beside him and said good morning.

"Oh. . . . Good morning," he said stiffly. He stood up, fastening the buckle of the case and giving it a pat as it swung into its usual facing-forward position on his stomach. "All set?"

"The others are not here yet. It's still early."

"Ah. No. Of course." He wiped his mustache carefully with his hand and tucked his chin back into his neck. "No bombs today, I hope?"

He wasn't altogether meaning to joke.

"No bombs," I assured him.

He nodded, not meeting my eyes. "Very upsetting, last Friday. Very upsetting, you know." He paused. "Nearly didn't come today, when I heard that Colin—er—" He stopped.

"I'll stay in the airplane all afternoon," I promised him.

The Major nodded again, sharply. "Had a Board of Trade fellow come to see me. Did you know that?"

"They told me so."

"Been to see you, too, I suppose."

"Yes."

"They get about a bit."

"They're very thorough. They'll go a hundred miles to get a single answer to a simple question."

He looked at me sharply. "Speaking from bitter experience?"

I hadn't known there was any feeling in my voice. I said, "I've been told they do."

He grunted. "Can't think why they don't leave it to the police."

No such luck, I thought. There was no police force in the world as tenacious as the British Board of Trade.

Annie Villars and Colin Ross arrived together, deep in a persuasive argument that was getting nowhere.

"Just say you'll ride my horses whenever you can."

". . . too many commitments."

"I'm not asking a great deal."

"There are reasons, Annie. Sorry, but no." He said it with an air of finality, and she looked startled and upset.

59

"Good morning," she said to me abstractedly. "Morning, Rupert."

"Morning, Annie," said the Major.

Colin Ross had achieved narrow pale-gray trousers and a blue open-necked shirt.

"Morning, Matt," he said.

The Major took a step forward, bristling like a terrier. "Did I hear you turning down Annie's proposition?"

"Yes, Major."

"Why?" he asked in an aggrieved tone. "Our money is as good as anyone else's, and her horses are always fit."

"I'm sorry, Major, but no. Just let's leave it at that."

The Major looked affronted and took Annie Villars off to see if the bar was open. Colin sighed and sprawled in a wooden armchair.

"God save me," he said, "from crooks."

I sat down, too. "She doesn't seem crooked to me."

"Who, Annie? She isn't really. Just not one-hundred-per-cent permanently scrupulous. No, it's that crummy slob Goldenberg that I don't like. She does what he says, a lot too much. I'm not taking indirect riding orders from him."

"Like Kenny Bayst?" I suggested.

He looked at me sideways. "The word gets around, I see. Kenny reckons he's well out of it. Well, I'm not stepping in." He paused reflectively. "The Board of Trade investigator who came to see me asked if I thought there was any significance in Bayst having cried off the return trip the other day."

"What did you say?"

"I said I didn't. Did you?"

"I confess I wondered, because he did go across to the airplane after the races, and he certainly felt murderous, but . . ."

"But," he agreed. "Would Kenny Bayst be cold-blooded enough to kill you and me as well?" He shook his head. "Not Kenny, I wouldn't have thought."

"And besides that," I said, nodding, "he only came to the steaming boil after he lost the three-thirty, and just how would he rustle up a bomb at Haydock in a little over one hour?"

"He would have to have arranged it in advance."

"That would mean that he knew he would lose the race. . . ."

"It's been done," said Colin dryly.

There was a pause. Then I said, "Anyway, I think we had it with us all the time. Right from before I left the base."

He swiveled his head and considered it. "In that case . . . Larry?"

"Would he?"

"God knows. Sneaky fellow. Pinched Nancy's hundred quid. But a bomb . . . And what was the point?"

I shook my head.

Colin said, "Bombs are usually either political or someone's next of kin wanting to collect the insurance."

"Fanatics or family . . ." I stifled the beginnings of a yawn.

"You don't really care, do you?" he said.

"Not that much."

"It doesn't disturb you enough to wonder whether the bomb merchant will try again?"

"About as much as it's disturbing you."

He grinned. "Yes . . . well. It would be handy to know for sure whose name was on that one. One would look so damn silly taking fiddly precautions if it was the Major who finally got clobbered. Or you."

"Me?" I said in astonishment.

"Why not?"

I shook my head. "I don't stand in anyone's way to anything."

"Someone may think you do."

"Then they're nuts."

"It takes a nut—a regular psycho—to put a bomb in an airplane."

Tyderman and Annie Villars came back from the direction of the bar with two more people, a man and a woman.

"Oh, Christ," Colin said under his breath. "Here

comes my own personal Chanter." He looked at me accusingly. "You didn't tell me who the other passengers were."

"I don't know them. Who are they? I don't do the bookings."

We stood up. The woman, who was in her thirties but dressed like a teen-ager, made a straight line for Colin and kissed him exuberantly on the cheek.

"Colin, darling, there was a spare seat and Annie said I could come. Wasn't that absolutely super of her?"

Colin glared at Annie, who pretended not to notice.

The girl-woman had a strong upper-class accent, white knee socks, a camel-colored high-waisted dress, several jingling gold bracelets, streaky long fair brown hair, a knock-you-down exotic scent, and an air of expecting everyone to curl up and die for her.

She latched her arm through Colin's so that he couldn't disentangle without giving offense, and said with a somehow unattractive gaiety, "Come along, everyone, let's take the plunge. Isn't it all just too unnerving, flying around with Colin these days?"

"You don't actually have to come," Colin said without quite disguising his wishes.

She seemed oblivious. "Darling," she said, "too riveting. Nothing would stop me."

She moved off toward the door, followed by the Major and Annie and the new man together, and finally by me. The new man was large and had the same air as the woman of expecting people to jump to it and smooth his path. The Major and Annie Villars were busy smoothing it, their ears bent deferentially to catch any falling crumbs of wisdom, their heads nodding in agreement over every opinion.

The two just-teen-age girls I had stationed beside the locked aircraft were still on duty, retained more by the promise of Colin's autographs than by my money. They got both, and were delighted. No one, they anxiously insisted, had even come close enough to ask what they were doing. No one could possibly have put a piece of chewing gum onto the airplane, let alone a bomb.

Colin, signing away, gave me a sidelong look of amusement and appreciation, and said safety came cheap at the price. He was less amused to find that the affectionate lady had stationed herself in one of the rear seats and was beckoning him to come and sit beside her.

"Who is she?" I asked.

"Fenella Payne-Percival. Fenella pain-in-the-neck."

I laughed. "And the man?"

"Duke of Wessex. Annie's got a horse running for him today."

"Not Rudiments again?"

He looked up in surprise from the second autograph book.

"Yes. That's right. Bit soon, I would have thought."

He finished the book and gave it back. "Kenny Bayst isn't riding it." His voice was dry.

"You don't say."

The passengers had sorted themselves out so that Annie and the Duke sat in the center seats, with the Major waiting beside the first two for me to get in before him. As I stepped up onto the wing he nodded his stiff little nod and pushed at his mustache. Less tense, slightly less rigid than last time. The owner was along instead of Goldenberg and Kenny wasn't there to stir things up. No coup today, I thought. No coup to go wrong.

The flight up was easy and uneventful, homing to the radio beacon on the coast at Ottringham and tracking away from it on a radial to Redcar. We landed without fuss on the racecourse, and the passengers yawned and unbuckled themselves.

"I wish every racecourse had a landing strip," Colin said with a sigh. "It makes the whole day so much easier. I hate all those dashes from airport to course by taxi."

The racecourses which catered to airplanes were in a minority, which seemed a shame considering there was room on most, if anyone cared enough. Harley

constantly raved in frustration at having to land ten
or fifteen miles away and fix up transportation for the
passengers. All the conveniently placed R.A.F. airfields
with superb runways that either refused to let private
aircraft land at all or shut their doors firmly at 5 P.M.
weekdays and all day on Saturdays had him on the
verge of tears. As also did the airfields whose owners
said they wouldn't take the responsibility of having
an aircraft land there or take off if they didn't have a
fire engine standing by, even though Harley's own
insurance didn't require it.

"The English are as air-minded as earthworms,"
Harley said.

On the other hand, Honey had tacked a list to the
office wall which started in big red letters "God Bless
. . ." and continued with all the friendly and accom-
modating places like Kempton Park, which let you
land up the five-furlong straight (except during five-
furlong races), and R.A.F. stations like Wroughton
and Leeming and Pershore, which really tried for
you, and the airfields that could let you land when
they were officially shut, and all the privately owned
strips whose owners generously agreed to your using
them any time you liked.

Harley's view of heaven was an open public landing
field outside every town and a wind sock and a flat
four furlongs on every racecourse. It wasn't much to
ask, he said plaintively. Not in view of the dozens of
enormous airfields which had been built during
World War II and were now disused and wasted.

He could dream, I thought. There was never any
money for such schemes, except in wars.

The passengers stretched themselves onto the
grass. Fenella Payne-Percival made little up and
down jumps of excitement like a small girl, the Major
patted his binocular case reassuringly, Annie Villars
efficiently picked up her own belongings and directed
a look of melting feminine helplessness toward the
Duke, Colin looked at his watch and smiled, and the
Duke himself glanced interestedly around and said,
"Nice day, what?"

64

A big man, he had a fine-looking head with thick graying hair, eyebrows beginning to sprout, and a strong square jaw, but there wasn't enough living stamped on his face for a man in his fifties, and I remembered what Nancy had said of him: sweet as they come, but nothing but cotton wool upstairs.

Colin said to me, "Are you coming into the paddock?"

I shook my head. "Better stay with the airplane this time."

The Duke said, "Won't you need some lunch, my dear chap?"

"It's kind of you, sir, but I often don't have any."

"Really?" He smiled. "Must have my lunch."

Annie Villars said, "We'll leave soon after the last. About a quarter to five."

"Right," I agreed.

"Doesn't give us time for a drink, Annie," complained the Duke.

She swallowed her irritation. "Any time after that, then."

"I'll be here," I said.

"Oh, do come on," said Fenella impatiently. "The pilot can look after himself, can't he? Let's get going, do. Come on, Colin, darling." She twined her arm in his again and he all but squirmed. They moved away toward the paddock obediently, with only Colin looking back. I laughed at the desperation on his face, and he stuck out his tongue.

There were three other aircraft parked in a row. One private, one from a Scottish taxi firm, and one Polyplane. All the pilots seemed to have gone into the races, but when I climbed out halfway through the afternoon to stretch my legs, I found the Polyplane pilot standing ten yards away, staring at the Cherokee with narrowed eyes and smoking a cigarette.

He was one of the two who had been at Haydock. He seemed surprised that I was there.

"Hello," I said equably. Always a sucker.

He gave me the old hard stare. "Taking no chances today, I see."

I ignored the sneer in his voice. "That's right."

"We got rid of that aircraft," he said sarcastically, nodding toward it, "because we'd flown the guts out of it. It's only suitable now for minor operators like you."

"It shows signs of the way you flew it," I agreed politely: and that deadly insult did nothing toward cooling the feud.

He compressed his lips and flicked the end of his cigarette away into the grass. A thin trickle of blue smoke arose from among the tangled green blades. I watched it without comment. He knew as well as I did that smoking near parked aircraft was incredibly foolish, and on all airfields forbidden.

He said, "I'm surprised you take the risk of flying Colin Ross. If your firm are proved to be responsible for his death, you'll be out of business."

"He's not dead yet."

"If I were him, I wouldn't risk flying any more with Derrydowns."

"Did he, by any chance," I asked, "once fly with Polyplanes? Is all this sourness due to his having transferred to Derrydowns instead?"

He gave me a bitter stare. "No," he said.

I didn't believe him. He saw that I didn't. He turned on his heel and walked away.

Rudiments won the big race. The dim green colors streaked up the center of the track at the last possible moment and pushed Colin on the favorite into second place. I could hear the boos all the way from the stands.

An hour until the end of racing. I yawned, leaned back in my seat, and went to sleep.

A young voice saying "Excuse me" several times woke me up. I opened my eyes. He was about ten, slightly shy, ultra-well bred. Squatting down on the wing, he spoke through the open door.

"I say, I'm sorry to wake you, but my uncle wanted me to come over and fetch you. He said you hadn't had anything to eat all day. He thinks you ought to. And besides he's had a winner and he wants you to drink his health."

"Your uncle is remarkably kind," I said, "but I can't leave the airplane."

"Well, actually, he thought of that. I've brought my father's chauffeur over with me, and he is going to sit here for you until you come back." He smiled with genuine satisfaction at these arrangements.

I looked past him out of the door, and there, sure enough, was the chauffeur, all togged up in the dark green with a shining peak to his cap.

"O.K.," I said. "I'll get my jacket."

He walked with me along to the paddock, through the gate, and across to the members' bar.

"Awfully nice chap, my uncle," he said.

"Unusually thoughtful," I agreed.

"Soft, my mother says," he said dispassionately. "He's her brother. They don't get along very well."

"What a pity."

"Oh, I don't know. If they were frightfully chummy, she would always be wanting to come with me when I go to stay with him. As it is, I go on my own, and we have some fantastic times, him and me. That's how I know how super he is." He paused. "Lots of people think he's terribly thick, I don't know why." There was a shade of anxiety in his young voice. "He's really awfully kind."

I reassured him. "I only met him this morning, but I think he's very nice."

His brow cleared. "You do? Oh, good."

The Duke was knee deep in cronies, all armed with glasses of champagne. His nephew disappeared from my side, dived through the throng, and reappeared tugging at his uncle's arm.

"What?" The kind brown eyes looked round; saw me. "Oh, yes." He bent down to talk, and presently the boy came back.

"Champagne or coffee?"

"Coffee, please."

"I'll get it for you."

"I'll get it," I suggested.

"No. Let me. Do let me. Uncle gave me the money." He marched off to the far end of the counter and ordered a cup of coffee and two rounds of smoked-salmon sandwiches, and paid for them with a well-crushed pound note.

"There," he said triumphantly. "How's that?"

"Fine," I said. "Terrific. Have a sandwich."

"All right."

We munched companionably.

"I say," he said. "Look at that man over there, he looks like a ghost."

I turned my head. Big blond man with very pale skin. Pair of clumsy crutches. Large plaster cast. Acey Jones.

Not so noisy today. Drinking beer very quietly in a far corner with a nondescript friend.

"He fell down some steps and broke his ankle and collected a thousand pounds from an insurance policy," I said.

"Golly," said the boy. "Almost worth it."

"He thinks so, too."

"Uncle has something to do with insurance. Don't know what, though."

"An underwriter?" I suggested.

"What's that?"

"Someone who invests money in insurance companies, in a special sort of way."

"He talks about Lloyd's, sometimes. Is it something to do with Lloyd's?"

"That's right."

He nodded and looked wistfully at the sandwiches.

"Have another," I suggested.

"They're yours, really."

"Go on. I'd like you to."

He gave me a quick bright glance and bit into Number 2.

"My name's Matthew," he said.

I laughed. "So is mine."

68

"Is it really? Do you really mean it?"

"Yes."

"Wow."

There was a step behind me and the deep Eton-sounding voice said, "Is Matthew looking after you all right?"

"Great, sir, thank you," I said.

"His name is Matthew, too," said the boy.

The Duke looked from one of us to the other. "A couple of Matts, eh? Don't let too many people wipe their feet on you."

Matthew thought it a great joke, but the touch of sadness in the voice was revealing. He was dimly aware that, despite his ancestry and position, one or two sharper types had wiped their feet on *him*.

I began to like the Duke.

"Well done with Rudiments, sir," I said.

His face lit up. "Splendid, wasn't it? Absolutely splendid. Nothing on earth gives me more pleasure than seeing my horses win."

I went back to the Cherokee just before the last race and found the chauffeur safe and sound reading *Doctor Zhivago*. He stretched, reported nothing doing, and ambled off.

All the same, I checked the aircraft inch by inch inside and even unscrewed the panel to the aft baggage compartment, so that I could see into the rear part of the fuselage, right back to the tail. Nothing there that shouldn't be. I screwed the panel on again.

Outside the aircraft, I started in the same way. Started only: because when I was examining every hinge in the tail plane, I heard a shout from the next aircraft.

I looked round curiously but without much haste.

Against that side of the Polyplane which faced away from the stands, two large men were laying into Kenny Bayst.

Chapter Six

The pilot of the Polyplane was standing aside and watching. I reached him in six strides.

"For God's sake," I said, "come and help him."

He gave me a cold stolid stare. "I've got my medical tomorrow. Do it yourself."

In three more steps, I caught one of the men by the fist as he lifted it high to smash into the crumpling Kenny, bent his arm savagely backward, and kicked him hard in the left hamstring. He fell over on his back with a shout of mixed anger, surprise, and pain, closely echoed in both emotion and volume by his colleague, who received the toe of my shoe very solidly at the base of his spine.

Bashing people was their sort of business, not mine, and Kenny hadn't enough strength left to stand up, let alone fight back, so that I got knocked about a bit here and there. But I imagined that they hadn't expected any serious opposition, and it must have been clear to them from the beginning that I didn't play their rules.

They had big fists all threateningly bunched and the hard round sort of toecaps which cowards hide behind. I kicked their knees with vigor, stuck my fingers out straight and hard toward their eyes, and chopped the sides of my palms at their throats.

I'd had enough of it before they had. Still, I outlasted them for determination, because I really did not want to fall down and have their boots bust my kidneys. They got tired in the end and limped away quite suddenly, as if called off by a whistle. They took with them some damaged knee cartilage, aching larynxes, and one badly scratched eye; and they left behind a ringing head and a set of sore ribs.

I leaned against the airplane, getting my breath back and looking down at Kenny where he sat on the grass. There was a good deal of blood on his face. His nose was bleeding, and he had tried to wipe it with the back of his hand.

I bent down presently and helped him up. He came to his feet without any of the terrible slowness of the severely injured and there was nothing wrong with his voice.

"Thanks, sport." He squinted at me. "Those sods said they were going to fix me so my riding days were over. . . . God . . . I feel crook. . . . Here, have you got any whisky? Aah . . . Jesus . . ." He bent double and vomited rackingly onto the turf.

Straightening up afterward, he dragged a large handkerchief out of his pocket and wiped his mouth, looking in dismay at the resulting red stains.

"I'm bleeding. . . ."

"It's your nose, that's all."

"Oh . . ." He coughed weakly. "Look, sport, thanks. I guess thanks isn't enough. . . ." His gaze sharpened on the Polyplane pilot still standing aloof a little way off. "That bastard didn't lift a finger. . . . They'd have crippled me and he wouldn't come. . . . I shouted."

"He's got his medical tomorrow," I said.

"Sod his bloody medical."

"If you don't pass your medical every six months, you get grounded. If you get grounded for long in the taxi business, you lose either your whole job or at least half your income. . . ."

"Yeah," he said. "And your own medical, when does that come up?"

"Not for two months."

He laughed a hollow, sick-sounding laugh. Swallowed. Swayed. Looked suddenly very small and vulnerable.

72

"You'd better go over and see the doctor," I suggested.

"Maybe . . . but I've got the ride on Volume Ten on Monday. . . . Big race . . . opportunity if I do well of a better job than I've had with Annie Villars. . . . Don't want to miss it. . . ." He smiled twistedly. "Doesn't do jockeys any good to be grounded either, sport."

"You're not in very good shape."

"I'll be all right. Nothing broken . . . except maybe my nose. That won't matter; done it before." He coughed again. "Hot bath. Spell in the sauna. Good as new by Monday. Thanks to you."

"How about telling the police?"

"Yeah. Great idea." He was sarcastic. "Just imagine their sort of questions. 'Why was anyone trying to cripple you, Mr. Bayst?' 'Well, Officer, I'd promised to fiddle their races, see, and this sod Goldenberg—I beg his pardon, gentlemen, Mr. Eric Goldenberg—sticks these two heavies onto me to get his own back for all the lolly he had to cough up when I won. . . .' 'And why did you promise to fiddle the race, Mr. Bayst?' 'Well, Officer, I done it before, you see, and made a handy bit on the side. . . .'" He gave me a flickering glance and decided he'd said enough. "Guess I'll see how it looks tomorrow. If I'm in shape to ride Monday, I'll just forget it happened."

"Suppose they try again?"

"No." He shook his head a fraction. "They don't do it twice."

He picked himself off the side of the fuselage and, looking at his reflection in the Polyplane's window, licked his handkerchief and wiped most of the blood off his face.

The nose had stopped bleeding. He felt it gingerly between thumb and forefinger.

"It isn't moving. Can't feel it grate. It did when I broke it."

Without the blood, he looked pale under the red hair but not leaden. "Guess I'll be all right. Think I'll get into the plane and sit down, though. . . . Came in it, see. . . ."

73

I helped him in. He sagged down weakly in his seat, and didn't look like someone who would be fit to ride a race horse in forty-six hours.

"Hey," he said, "I never asked you. . . . Are you O.K. yourself?"

"Yes. . . . Look, I'll get your pilot to fetch you some whisky."

His reaction showed how unsettled he still felt. "That would be . . . fair dinkum. He won't go, though."

"He will," I said.

He did. British aviation was a small world. Everyone knew someone who knew someone else. News of certain sorts traveled slowly but surely outward and tended to follow one around. He got the message. He also agreed to buy the whisky himself.

By the time he came back, bearing a full quarter bottle and a scowl, the last race was over and the passengers for all the airplanes were turning up in little groups. Kenny began to look less shaky, and when two other jockeys arrived with exclamations and consolations, I went back to the Cherokee.

Annie Villars was waiting, not noticeably elated by her win with Rudiments.

"I thought you said you were going to stay with the plane," she said. Ice crackled in her voice.

"Didn't take my eyes off it."

She snorted. I did a quick double check inside, just to be sure, but no one had stored anything aboard since my last search. The external check I did more slowly and thoroughly. Still nothing.

The thumping I'd collected started to catch up. The ringing noise in my head was settling into a heavy ache. Various soggy areas on my upper arms were beginning to stiffen. My solar plexus and adjacent areas felt like Henry Cooper's opponent's on the morning after.

"Did you know," I said to Annie Villars conversationally, "that two men just had a go at beating up Kenny Bayst?"

If she felt any compassion, she controlled it admirably. "Is he badly hurt?"

"An uncomfortable night should see him through."

"Well, then . . . I dare say he deserved it."

"What for?"

She gave me a direct stare. "You aren't deaf."

I shrugged. "Kenny thinks Mr. Goldenberg arranged it."

She hadn't known it was going to happen. Didn't know whether Goldenberg was responsible or not. I saw her hesitating, summing the information up.

In the end, she said. vaguely, "Kenny never could keep his tongue still," and a minute later, under her breath, "Stupid thing to do. Stupid man."

Major Tyderman, the Duke of Wessex, and Fenella Payne-in-the-neck arrived together, the Duke still talking happily about his winner.

"Where's Colin?" asked Fenella. "Isn't he here, after all? What a frantic nuisance. I asked for him at the weighing room and that man—who did he say he was? His valet—oh, yes, of course. . . . His valet said that he had already gone to the plane." She pouted, thrusting out her lower lip. There was champagne in her eyes and petulance in her voice. The gold bracelets jingled. The heavy scent didn't seem to have abated during the afternoon. I thought Colin had dodged very neatly. The Major had also been included in the celebrations. He looked slightly fuzzy round the eyes and a lot less rigid everywhere else. The hand that pushed at the wiry mustache looked almost gentle. The chin was still tucked well back into the neck, but there was nothing aggressive any more: it seemed suddenly only the mannerism of one who used suspiciousness instead of understanding to give himself a reputation for shrewdness.

The Duke asked the Major if he minded changing places on the way home so that he, the Duke, could sit in front. "I like to see the dials go round," he explained.

The Major, full of ducal champagne, gracefully

agreed. He and Fenella climbed aboard and I waited outside with the Duke.

"Is there anything the matter, my dear chap?" he said.

"No, sir."

He studied me slowly. "There is, you know."

I put my fingers on my forehead and felt the sweat. "It's a hot day," I said.

Colin came eventually. He, too, was sweating: his crumpled open shirt had great dark patches under the arms. He had ridden five races. He looked thin and exhausted.

"Are you all right?" he said abruptly.

"I *knew*," said the Duke.

"Yes, thank you."

Colin looked back to where the Polyplane still waited on the ground.

"Is Kenny bad?"

"A bit sore. He didn't want anyone to know."

"One of the jockeys with him on the trip came back over and told us. Kenny said you saved him from a fate worse than death, or words to that effect."

"What?" said the Duke.

Colin explained. They looked at me anxiously.

"I'm fit to fly, if that's what's worrying you."

Colin made a face. "Yeah, boy, it sure is." He grinned, took a deep breath, and dived into the back with the tentacled Fenella. The Duke folded himself after me into the front seat and we set off.

There was thick cloud over the Humber at Ottringham and all the way south to Cambridge. As he could see just about as far forward as the propeller, the Duke asked me what guarantee there was that we wouldn't collide with another aircraft.

There wasn't any guarantee. Just probability.

"The sky is huge," I said. "And there are strict rules for flying in clouds. Collisions practically never happen."

His hands visibly relaxed. He shifted into a more comfortable position. "How do you know where we are?" he asked.

"Radio," I said. "Radio beams from transmitters on the ground. As long as that needle on the dial points centrally downward, we are going straight to Ottringham, where the signal is coming from."

"Fascinating," he said.

The replacement Cherokee had none of the sophistication of the one which had been blown up. That had had an instrument which locked the steering onto the radio beam and took the aircraft automatically to the transmitter. After the attentions of Kenny Bayst's assailants, I regretted not having it around.

"How will we know when we get to Cambridge?" asked the Duke.

"The needle on that other dial there will swing from pointing straight up and point straight down. That will mean we have passed over the top of the transmitter at Cambridge."

"Wonderful what they think of," said the Duke.

The needles came up trumps. We let down through the cloud over Cambridge into an overcast angry-looking afternoon and landed on the shower-soaked tarmac. I taxied them over close to the buildings, shut down the engine, and took off my headset, which felt a ton heavier than usual.

"Wouldn't have missed it," said the Duke. "Always motored everywhere before, you know." He unfastened his safety belt. "Annie persuaded me to try flying. Just once, she said. But I'll be coming with you again, my dear chap."

"That's great, sir."

He looked at me closely, kindly. "You want to go straight to bed when you get home, Matthew. Get your wife to tuck you up nice and warm, eh?"

"Yes," I said.

"Good, good." He nodded his fine head and began to heave himself cumbersomely out of the door and onto the wing. "You made a great hit with my nephew, my dear chap. And I respect Matt's opinion. He can spot good'uns and bad'uns a mile off."

"He's a nice boy," I said.

The Duke smiled happily. "He's my heir."

77

He stepped down from the wing and went round to help Annie Villars put on her coat. No doubt I should have been doing it. I sat with my belt still fastened, feeling too rough to be bothered to move. I didn't relish the thought of the final hop back to Buckingham, up into the clouds again and with no easy well-placed transmitter to help me down at the other end. I'd have to go round the Luton complex. . . . Could probably get a steer home from there, from the twenty-four-hour radar at Bedford. . . .

I ached. I thought of the caravan. Cold little harbor.

The passengers collected their gear, shut the rear door, waved and walked off toward the buildings. I looked at the map, picked out a heading, planned the return journey in terms of time and the cross references I'd need to tell me when I'd got to Buckingham, if the radar should be out of service. After that, I sat and stared at the flight plan and told myself to get on with it. After that, I rested my head on my hand and shut my eyes.

Ridiculous wasting time, I thought. Cambridge Airport charged extra for every minute they stayed open after five o'clock, and the passengers were already committed to paying for a couple of hours. Every moment I lingered cost them a little more.

There was a tap on the window beside me. I raised my head more quickly than proved wise. Colin Ross was standing there, watching me with a gleam of humor. I twisted the catch and opened the window flap on its hinge.

"Fit to fly, didn't you say?" he said.

"That was two hours ago."

"Ah, yes. Makes a difference." He smiled faintly. "I just wondered, if you don't feel like going on, whether you'd care to let me take you home for the night? Then you can finish the trip tomorrow. It might be a fine day tomorrow."

He had flown a great deal and understood the difficulties. All the same, I was surprised he had troubled to come back.

"It might," I agreed. "But I could stay in Cambridge. . . ."

"Get out of there and fix the hangarage," he said calmly.

"I'll have to check with Derrydowns. . . ."

"Check, then."

I climbed too slowly out of the airplane and struggled into my jacket. We walked together across into the building.

"Call your wife, too," he said.

"Haven't got one."

"Oh." He looked at me with speculative curiosity.

"No," I said. "Not that. Married twelve years, divorced three."

Humor crinkled the skin round his eyes. "Better than me," he said. "Married two years, divorced four."

Harley answered at the first ring.

"Where are you? Cambridge? . . . No, come back now. If you stay at Cambridge, we'll have to pay the hangarage." I hadn't told him about the fight, about the way I felt.

"I'll pay it," I said. "You can deduct it from my salary. Colin Ross has asked me to stay with him." That would clinch it. Harley saw the importance of pleasing, and Colin Ross was his best customer.

"Oh . . . that's different. All right, then. Come back in the morning."

I went into the control office and arranged for the aircraft to be stowed under cover for the night, one last overtime job for the staff before they all went home. After that, I sank into the Ross Aston Martin and let the world take care of itself.

He lived in an ordinary-looking brick-built bungalow on the outskirts of Newmarket. Inside, it was colorful and warm, with a large sitting room stocked with deep luxurious velvet-upholstered armchairs.

"Sit down," he said.

I did. Put my head back. Shut my eyes.

79

"Whisky or brandy?" he asked.

"Whichever you like."

I heard him pouring. It sounded like a tumblerful.

"Here," he said.

I opened my eyes and gratefully took the glass. It was brandy-and-water. It did a grand job.

There were sounds of pans from the kitchen and a warm smell of roasting chicken. Colin's nose twitched.

"Dinner will be ready soon. . . . I'll go and tell the cooks there will be one extra."

He went out of the room and came back almost immediately with his two cooks.

I stood up slowly. I hadn't given it a thought, was quite unprepared.

They looked at first sight like two halves of one whole: Nancy and Midge. Same dark hair, tied high on the crown with black velvet bows. Same dark eyes, straight eyebrows, spontaneous smiles.

"The birdman himself," Nancy said. "Colin, how did you snare him?"

"Potted a sitting duck. . . ."

"This is Midge," she said. "Midge . . . Matt."

"Hi," she said. "The bomb man, aren't you?"

When you looked closer, you could see. She was thinner than Nancy, and much paler, and she seemed fragile where Nancy was strong: but without the mirror comparison with her sister there was no impression of her being ill.

"First and last bomb, I hope," I said.

She shivered. "A lot too ruddy close."

Colin poured each of them a Dubonnet and took whisky for himself. "Bombs, battles—some introduction you've had to racing."

"An eventful change from crop spraying," I said.

"Is that a dull job?" Midge asked, surprised.

"Dull and dangerous. You get bored to death trudging up and down some vast field for six hours a day. It's all low flying, you see, so you have to be wide awake, and after a while you start yawning. One day maybe you get careless and touch the ground with your wing in a turn, and you write off an expensive machine, which is apt to be unpopular with the boss."

Nancy laughed. "Is that what you did?"

"No. . . . I went to sleep for a second in the air one day and woke up twenty feet from a pylon. Missed it by millimeters. So I quit while everything was still in one piece."

"Never mind," Midge said. "The next plane you touched disintegrated beautifully."

They laughed together, a united family, close.

Colin told them about Kenny Bayst's fracas and they exclaimed sympathetically, which made me feel a humbug: Colin habitually drove himself to exhaustion and Midge was irretrievably afflicted, and all I had were a few minor bruises.

Dinner consisted simply of the hot roast chicken and a tossed green salad, with thick wedges of cheese afterward. We ate in the kitchen with our elbows on the scarlet table, and chewed the chicken bones. I hadn't passed a more basically satisfying evening for many a long weary year.

"What are you thinking?" Nancy demanded. "At this moment?"

"Making a note to fall frequently sick at Cambridge."

"Well," said Midge. "Don't bother. Just come any time." She looked inquiringly at her sister and brother, and they nodded. "Just come," she repeated. "Whenever it's handy."

The old inner warning raised its urgent head: don't get involved, don't feel anything, don't risk it.

Don't get involved.

I said, "Nothing I'd like better," and didn't know whether I meant it or not.

The two girls stacked the plates in a dishwasher and made coffee. Nancy poured cream carefully across the top of her cup.

"Do you think that bomb was really intended for Colin?" she asked suddenly.

I shrugged. "I don't know. It could just as well have been intended for Major Tyderman or Annie Villars or Goldenberg, or even Kenny Bayst, really, because it must have been on board before he decided not to come. Or it might have been intended for putting the firm out of action—for Derrydowns itself, if you see what I mean, because if Colin had been killed, Derrydowns would probably have gone bust."

"I can't see why anyone would want to kill Colin," Midge said. "Sure, people are jealous of him, but jealousy is one thing and killing five people is another. . . ."

"Everyone seems to be taking it so calmly," Nancy suddenly exploded. "Here is this bloody bomb merchant running around loose with no one knowing just what he'll do next, and no one seems to be trying to find out and lock him up."

"I don't see how they can find him," Colin said. "And anyway I don't suppose he will risk trying it again."

"Oh, you—you—*ostrich*," she said bitterly. "Doesn't it occur to you that you don't just lightly put a bomb in an airplane? Whoever did it must have had an overwhelming reason, however mad it was, and since the whole thing went wrong they still have the same motive rotting away inside them, and what do you think Midge and I will do if next time you get blown to bits?"

I saw Midge looking at her with compassion and understood the extent of Nancy's fear. One day she was certainly going to lose her sister. She couldn't face losing her brother as well.

"It won't happen," he said calmly.

They looked at him, and at me. There was a long, long pause. Then Midge picked up the wishbone of the chicken and held it out for me to pull. It snapped with the bigger side in her fist.

"I wish," she said seriously, "that Colin would stop cutting his toenails in the bath."

Chapter Seven

I slept on a divan bed in Colin's study, a small room crammed with racing trophies, filing cabinets, and form books. Every wall was lined with rows of framed photographs of horses passing winning posts and owners proudly leading them in. Their hoofs thudded through my head most of the night, but all was peace by morning.

Colin brought me a cup of tea, yawning in his dark woolly bathrobe. He put the cup down on the small table beside the divan and pulled back the curtains.

"It's drizzling cats and dogs," he announced. "There's no chance of you flying this morning, so you may as well relax and go back to sleep."

I looked out at the misty rain. Didn't mind a bit.

"It's my day off," I said.

"Couldn't be better."

He perched his bottom on the edge of the desk.

"Are you O.K. this morning?"

"Fine," I said. "That hot bath loosened things a lot."

"Every time you moved yesterday evening, you could see it hurt."

I made a face. "Sorry."

"Don't be. In this house, you say ouch."

"So I've noticed," I said dryly.

He grinned. "Everyone lives on a precipice. All the time. And Midge keeps telling me and Nancy that if we're not careful she'll outlive us both."

"She's marvelous."

"Yes, she is." He looked out of the window. "It was a terrible shock at first. Terrible. But now . . . I don't know . . . we seem to have accepted it. All of us. Even her."

I said hesitantly, "How long? . . ."

"How long will she live? No one knows. It varies so much, apparently. She's had it, they think, for about three years now. It seems a lot of people have it for about a year before it becomes noticeable enough to be diagnosed, so no one knows when it started with Midge. Some people die within days of getting it. Some have lived for twenty years. Nowadays, with all the modern treatments, they say the average after diagnosis is from two to six years, but it will possibly be ten. We've had two. . . . We just believe it will be ten . . . and that makes it much easier. . . ."

"She doesn't look especially ill."

"Not at the moment. She had pneumonia a short while ago, and the odd thing about that is that it reverses leukemia for a while. Any fever does it, apparently. Actually makes her better. So do doses of radiation on her arms and legs, and other bones and organs. She's had several relapses and several good long spells of being well. It just goes on like that. . . . But her blood is different, and her bones are changing inside all the time—I've seen pictures of what is happening—and one day . . . Well, one day she'll have a sort of extreme relapse, and she won't recover."

"Poor Midge. . . ."

"Poor all of us."

"What about . . . Nancy? Being her twin . . ."

"Do identical bodies get identical blood diseases, do you mean?" He looked at me across the room, his eyes in shadow. "There's that, too. They say the chances are infinitesimal. They say there are only eighteen known cases of leukemia occurring twice in the same family unit. You can't catch it, and you can't inherit it. A girl with leukemia can have a baby, and the baby won't have leukemia. You can transfuse blood from someone with leukemia into someone without it, and he won't catch it. They say there's no reason why Nancy should develop it any more than me or you or the postman. But they don't *know*. The books don't record any cases of an identical twin having it, or what became of the other one." He paused. Swallowed. "I think we are all more afraid of Nancy getting it, too, than of anything on earth."

I stayed until the sky cleared up at five o'clock. Colin spent most of the day working out which races he wanted to ride in during the coming week and answering telephone calls from owners and trainers anxious to engage him. Principally he rode for a stable half a mile down the road, he said, but the terms of his retainer there gave him a good deal of choice.

He worked at a large chart with seven columns, one for each day of the week. Under each day he listed the various meetings, and under each meeting he listed the names, prizes, and distances of the races. Toward the end of the afternoon, there was a horse's name against a fair proportion of races, especially, I noticed, those with the highest rewards.

He grinned at my interest. "A business is a business," he said.

"So I see. A study in time and motion."

On three of the days, he proposed to ride at two meetings.

"Can you get me from Brighton to Windsor fast enough for two races an hour and a half apart? Three-o'clock race at Brighton. Four-thirty Windsor. And on Saturday three-o'clock race at Bath, four-thirty at Brighton?"

"With fast cars both ends, don't see why not."

"Good." He crossed out a couple of question marks and wrote ticks instead. "And next Sunday can you take me to France?"

"If Harley says so."

"Harley will say so," he said with certainty.

"Don't you ever take a day off?"

85

He raised his eyebrows in surprise. "Today," he said, "is off. Hadn't you noticed?"

"Er . . . yes."

"The horse I was going over to ride today went lame on Thursday. Otherwise I was going to Paris. B.E.A., though, for once."

Nancy said with mock resignation, "The dynamo whirs nonstop from March to November in England and Europe, and then goes whizzing off to Japan and so on, and around about February there might be a day or two when we can all flop back in armchairs and put our feet up."

Midge said, "We put them up in the Bahamas last time. It was gorgeous. All that hot sun . . ."

The others laughed. "It rained the whole of the first week."

The girls cooked steaks for lunch. "In your honor," Midge said to me. "You're too thin."

I was fatter than any of them; which wasn't saying much.

Midge cleared the things away afterward and Nancy covered the kitchen table with maps and charts.

"I really am flying Colin to the races one day soon, and I wondered if you'd help. . . ."

"Of course."

She bent over the table, the long dark hair swinging down over her neck. Don't get involved, I said to myself. Just don't.

"Next week, to Haydock. If the weather's good enough."

"She's doing you out of a job," Midge observed, wiping glasses.

"Wait till it thunders."

"Beast," Nancy said.

She had drawn a line on the map. She wanted me to tell her how to proceed in the Manchester control zone, and what to do if they gave her instructions she didn't understand.

"Ask them to repeat them. If you still don't understand, ask them to clarify."

"They'll think I'm stupid," she protested.

"Better that than barging on regardless and crashing into an airliner."

"O.K." She sighed. "Point taken."

"Colin deserves a medal," Midge said.

"Just shut up," Nancy said. "You're all bloody rude."

When the drizzle stopped, they all three took me back to Cambridge, squashing into the Aston Martin. Midge drove, obviously enjoying it. Nancy sat half on Colin and half on me, and I sat half on the door handle.

They stood in a row, and waved when I took off. I rolled the wings in salute and set course for Buckingham, and tried to ignore the regret I felt to be leaving.

Honey was up in the control tower at Derrydowns, Sunday or no Sunday, and Harley was aloft in the trainer giving someone a lesson. When he heard me on the radio, he said snappily "And about time, too," and I remembered the dimensions of my bank balance and didn't snap back. Chanter, I thought wryly, would have plain despised me.

I left the Cherokee Six in the hangar and walked round to the caravan. It seemed emptier, more sordid, more dilapidated than before. The windows all needed cleaning. The bed wasn't made. Yesterday's milk had gone sour again, and there was still no food.

I sat for a while watching the evening sun struggle through the breaking clouds, watching Harley's pupil stagger through some ropy landings, wondering how long it would be before Derrydowns went broke, and wondering if I could save enough before that happened to buy a car. Harley was paying me forty-five pounds a week, which was more than he could afford and less than I was worth. Of that, Susan, taxes, and insurance would be taking exactly half, and with Harley deducting four more for my rent it wasn't going to be easy.

Impatiently I got up and cleaned all the windows,

which improved my view of the airfield but not of the future.

When the light began to fade, I had a visitor. A ripe shapely girl in a minimum of green cotton dress. Long fair hair. Long legs. Large mouth. Slightly protruding teeth. She walked with a maneating sway and spoke with the faintest of lisps.

Honey Harley had come down from the tower.

She knocked on her way in. All the same if I'd been naked. As it was, I had my shirt off from the window cleaning, and for Honey, it seemed, that was invitation enough. She came over holding out a paper in one hand and putting the other lightly on my shoulder. She let it slide down against my skin to halfway down my back and then brought it up again to the top.

"Uncle and I were making out the list for next week. We wondered if you fixed anything up with Colin Ross."

I moved gently away, picked up a nylon sweater, and put it on.

"Yes. . . . He wants us Tuesday, Friday, Saturday, and Sunday."

"Great."

She followed me across the small space. One step further backward and I'd be in my bedroom. Internally I tried to stifle a laugh. I stepped casually round her, back toward the door. Her face showed nothing but businesslike calm.

"Look," she said, "Monday, that's tomorrow, then, you collect a businessman at Coventry, take him to Rotterdam, wait for him, and bring him back. That's in the Aztec. Tuesday, Colin Ross. Wednesday, nothing yet. Thursday, probably a trainer in Lambourn wanting to look at a horse for sale in Yorkshire—he'll let us know—and then Colin Ross again all the end of the week."

"O.K."

"And the Board of Trade want to come out and see

you again. I told them early Tuesday or Wednesday."

"All right." As usual, the automatic sinking of the heart even at the words "Board of Trade": though this time, surely, surely, my responsibility was a technicality. This time, surely, I couldn't get ground to bits.

Honey sat down on the two-seat sofa and crossed her legs. She smiled.

"We haven't seen much of each other yet, have we?"

"No," I said.

"Can I have a cigarette?"

"I'm sorry. . . . I don't smoke. . . . I haven't any."

"Oh. Well, give me a drink, then."

"Look, I really am sorry. . . . All I can offer you is black coffee . . . or water."

"Surely you've got some beer?"

"Afraid not."

She stared at me. Then she stood up, went into the tiny kitchen and opened all the cupboards. I thought it was because she thought I was lying, but I'd done her an injustice. Sex-minded she might be, but no fool.

"You've no car, have you? And the shops and the pub are nearly two miles away." She came back frowning, and sat down again. "Why didn't you ask someone to give you a lift?"

"Didn't want to be a bother."

She considered it. "You've been here three weeks and you don't get paid until the end of the month. So . . . have you any money?"

"Enough not to starve," I said. "But thanks all the same."

I'd sent ten pounds to Susan and told her she'd have to wait for the rest until I got my check. She'd written back short and to the point. Two months, by then, don't forget. As if I could. I now had under four pounds left in the world and too much pride.

"Uncle would give you an advance."

"I wouldn't like to ask him."

A small smile lifted the corners of her mouth. "No,

89

I can see that, as he's so intent on slapping you down."

"Is he?"

"Don't pretend to be surprised. You know he is. You give him a frightful inferiority complex and he's getting back at you for it."

"It's silly."

"Oh, sure. But you are the two things he longs to be and isn't, a top-class pilot and an attractive man. He needs you badly for the business, but he doesn't have to like it. And don't tell me you didn't know all this, because it's been obvious all along that you understand; otherwise you would have lost your temper with him every day at the treatment he's been handing out."

"You see a lot from your tower," I said, smiling.

"Sure. And I'm very fond of my uncle. And I love this little business, and I'd do anything to keep us afloat." She said it with intense feeling. I wondered whether "anything" meant sleeping with the pilots, or whether that came under the heading of pleasure, not profit. I didn't intend to find out. Not getting involved included Honey, in the biggest possible way.

I said, "It must have been a blow to the business, losing that new Cherokee."

She pursed her mouth and put her head on one side. "Not altogether. In fact, absolutely the reverse. We had too much capital tied up in it. We had to put down a lump sum to start with, and the H.P. installments were pretty steep. . . . I should think when everything's settled, and we get the insurance, we will have about five thousand pounds back, and with that much to shore us up we can keep going until times get better."

"If the aircraft hadn't blown up, would you have been able to keep up with the H.P.?"

She stood up abruptly, seeming to think that she had already said too much. "Let's just leave it that things are all right as they are."

The daylight was fading fast. She came and stood close beside me, not quite touching.

"You don't smoke, you don't eat, you don't drink," she said softly. "What else don't you do?"

"That, too."

"Not ever?"

"Not now. Not here."

"I'd give you a good time."

"Honey . . . I just . . . don't want to."

She wasn't angry. Not even hurt. "You're cold," she said judiciously. "An iceberg."

"Perhaps."

"You'll thaw," she said. "One of these days."

The Board of Trade had sent the same two men, the tall one and the silent one, complete with note-book and bitten green pencil. As before, I sat with them in the crew room and offered them coffee from the slot machine in the passengers' lounge. They accepted, and I went and fetched three plastic cupfuls. The staff, as well as the customers, had to buy their coffee or whatever from the machine. Honey kept it well stocked. It made a profit.

Outside on the airfield my part-time colleague, Ron, was showing a new pupil how to do the external checks. They crept round the trainer inch by inch. Ron talked briskly. The pupil, a middleaged man, nodded as if he understood.

The tall man was saying in effect that they had got nowhere with the bomb.

"The police have been happy to leave the investigation with us, but frankly in these cases it is almost impossible to find the identity of the perpetrator. Of course, if someone on board is a major political figure, or a controversial agitator . . . Or if there is a great sum of personal insurance involved . . . But in this case there is nothing like that."

"Isn't Colin Ross insured?" I asked.

"Yes, but he has no new policy, or anything exceptional. And the beneficiaries are his twin sisters. I cannot believe . . ."

"Impossible," I said with conviction.

91

"Quite so."

"How about the others?"

He shook his head. "They all said, in fact, that they ought to be better insured than they were." He coughed discreetly. "There is, of course, the matter of yourself."

"What d'you mean?"

His sharp eyes stared at me unblinkingly.

"Several years ago, you took out a policy for the absolute benefit of your wife. Although she is now your ex-wife, she would still be the beneficiary. You can't change that sort of policy."

"Who told you all this?"

"She did," he said. "We went to see her in the course of our inquiries." He paused. "She didn't speak kindly of you."

I compressed my mouth. "No. I can imagine. Still, I'm worth more to her alive than dead. She'll want me to live as long as possible."

"And if she wanted to get married again? Your alimony payments would stop then, and a lump sum from insurance might be welcome."

I shook my head. "She might have killed me in a fury three years ago, but not now, cold-bloodedly, with other people involved. It isn't her nature. And besides she doesn't know anything about bombs and she had no opportunity. . . . You'll have to cross out that theory, too."

"She has been going out occasionally with an executive from a firm specializing in demolitions."

He kept his voice dead even, but he had clearly expected more reaction than he got. I wasn't horrified or even much taken aback.

"She wouldn't do it. Or put anyone else up to doing it. Ordinarily, she was too—too kindhearted. Too sensible, anyway. She used to be so angry whenever innocent passengers were blown up. . . . She would never do it herself. Never."

He watched me for a while in the special Board of Trade brand of unnerving silence. I didn't see what I could add. Didn't know what he was after.

Outside on the airfield, the trainer started up and taxied away. The engine noise faded. It was very quiet. I sat. I waited.

Finally he stirred. "All in all, for all our trouble, we have come up with only one probability. And even that gets us no nearer knowing who the bomb was intended for, or who put it on board."

He put his hand in his inner pocket and brought out a stiff brown envelope. Out of that he shook onto the crew-room table a twisted piece of metal. I picked it up and looked at it. Beyond the impression that it had once been round and flat, like a button, it meant nothing.

"What is it?"

"The remains," he said, "of an amplifier."

I looked up, puzzled. "Out of the radio?"

"We don't think so." He chewed his lip. "We think it was in the bomb. We found it embedded in what had been the tail plane."

"Do you mean . . . it wasn't a time bomb after all?"

"Well . . . probably not. It looks as if it was exploded by a radio transmission. Which puts, do you see, a different slant on things."

"What difference? I don't know much about bombs. How does a radio bomb differ from a time bomb?"

"They can differ a lot, though in many the actual explosive is the same. In those cases, it's just the trigger mechanism that's different." He paused. "Well, say you have a quantity of plastic explosive. Unfortunately that's all too easy to get hold of nowadays. In fact, if you happen to be in Greece, you can go into any hardware shop and buy it over the counter. On its own, it won't explode. It needs a detonator. Gunpowder, old-fashioned gunpowder, is the best. You also need something to ignite the gunpowder before it will detonate the plastic. Are you with me?"

"Faint but pursuing," I said.

"Right. The easiest way to ignite gunpowder—from a distance, that is—is to pack it round a thin filament of fuse wire. Then you pass an electric current through the filament. It becomes red hot, ignites the gunpowder—"

"And, boom, you have no Cherokee Six."

"Er, yes. Now, in this type of bomb you have a battery, a high-voltage battery about the size of a sixpence, to provide the electric current. The filament will heat up if you bend it round and fasten one end to one terminal of the battery, and the other to the other."

"Clear," I said. "And the bomb goes off immediately."

He raised his eyes to heaven. "Why did I ever start this? Yes, it would go off immediately. So it is necessary to have a mechanism that will complete the circuit after the manufacturer is safely out of the way."

"By a spring?" I suggested.

"Yes. You hold the circuit open by a hairspring on a catch. When the catch is removed, the spring snaps the circuit shut, and that's that. Right? Now, the catch can be released by a time mechanism like an ordinary alarm clock. Or it can be released by a radio signal from a distance, via a receiver, an amplifier, and a solenoid, like mechanisms in a space craft."

"What is a solenoid, exactly?"

"A sort of electric magnet, a coil with a rod in the center. The rod moves up and down inside the coil when a pulse is passed through the coil. Say the top of the rod is sticking up out of the coil to form the catch on the spring, when the rod moves down into the coil the spring is released."

I considered it. "What is there to stop someone detonating the bomb by accident, by unknowingly transmitting on the right frequency? The air is packed with radio waves—surely radio bombs are impossibly risky?"

He cleared his throat. "It is possible to make a combination-type release mechanism. One could make a bomb in which, say, three radio signals had to be completed. For such a release mechanism, you would need three separate sets of receivers, amplifiers, and solenoids to complete the circuit. . . . We were exceptionally fortunate to find this amplifier. We doubt if it was the only one. . . ."

"It sounds much more complicated than the alarm clock."

"Oh, yes, it is. But also more flexible. You are not committed to a time in advance to set it off."

"So no one had to know what time we would be leaving Haydock. They would just have to see us go."

"Yes. . . . Or be told you had gone."

I thought a bit. "It does put a different slant, doesn't it?"

"I'd appreciate your thinking."

"You must be thinking the same," I said. "If the bomb could be set off at any hour, any day—any week, even—it could have been put in the aircraft at any time after the last maintenance check."

He smiled thinly. "And that would let you halfway off the hook?"

"Halfway," I agreed.

"But only half."

"Yes."

He sighed. "I've sprung this on you. I'd like you to think it over, from every angle. Seriously. Then tell me if anything occurs to you. If you care at all to find out what happened, that is, and maybe prevent it from happening again."

"You think I don't care?"

"I got that impression."

"I would care now," I said slowly, "if Colin Ross were blown up."

He smiled. "You are less on your guard today."

"You aren't sniping at me from behind the bushes."

"No. . . ." He was surprised. "You're very observant, aren't you?"

"More a matter of atmosphere."

He hesitated. "I have now read the whole of the transcript of your trial."

"Oh." I could feel my face go bleak. He watched me.

"Did you know," he said, "that someone has added

95

to the bottom of it in pencil a highly libelous statement?"

"No," I said. Waited for it.

"It says the Chairman of Interport is of the undoubtedly correct opinion that the first officer lied on oath throughout, and that it was because of the first officer's own gross negligence, not that of Captain Shore, that the airliner strayed so dangerously off course."

Surprised, shaken, I looked away from him, out of the window, feeling absurdly vindicated and released. If that postscript was there for anyone who read the transcript to see, then maybe my name hadn't quite so much mud on it as I'd thought. Not where it mattered, anyway.

I said without heat, "The captain is always responsible. Whoever does what."

"Yes."

A silence lengthened. I brought my thoughts back from four years ago and my gaze from the empty airfield.

"Thank you," I said.

He smiled very slightly. "I wondered why you hadn't lost your license—or your job. It didn't make sense to me that you hadn't. That's why I read the transcript, to see if there was any reason."

"You're very thorough."

"I like to be."

"Interport knew one of us was lying—we both said the other had put the ship in danger—but I was the captain. It inevitably came back to me. It was, in fact, my fault."

"He willfully disobeyed your instructions. . . ."

"And I didn't find out until it was nearly too late."

"Quite . . . but he needn't have lied about it."

"He was frightened." I sighed. "Of what would happen to his career."

He let half a minute slip by without comment. Then he cleared his throat and said, "I suppose you wouldn't like to tell me why you left the South American people?"

I admired his delicate approach. "Gap in the dossier?" I suggested.

His mouth twitched. "Well, yes." A pause. "You are of course not obliged. . . ."

"No." I said. "Still . . ." Something for something. "I refused to take off one day because I didn't think it was safe. They got another pilot who said it was. So he took off, and nothing happened. And they sacked me. That's all."

"But," he said blankly, "it's a captain's absolute right not to take off if he thinks it's unsafe."

"There's no B.A.L.P.A. to uphold your rights there, you know. They said they couldn't afford to lose custom to other airlines because their captains were cowards. Or words to that effect."

"Good gracious."

I smiled. "Probably the Interport business accounted for my refusal to take risks."

"But then you went to Africa and took them," he protested.

"Well . . . I needed money badly, and the pay was fantastic. And you don't have the same moral obligation to food and medical supplies as to airline passengers."

"But the refugees and wounded, coming out?"

"Always easier flying out than in. No difficulties finding the home base, not like groping for some jungle clearing on a black night."

He shook his head wonderingly, giving me up as a bad job.

"What brought you back here to something as dull as crop spraying?"

I laughed. Never thought I could laugh in front of the Board of Trade. "The particular war I was flying in ended. I was offered another one a bit further south, but I suppose I'd had enough of it. Also I was nearly solvent again. So I came back here, and crop spraying was the first thing handy."

"What you might call a checkered career," he commented.

"Mild compared with some."

97

"Ah, yes. That's true." He stood up and threw his empty coffee beaker into the biscuit tin which served as a waste-paper basket. "Right, then. . . . You'll give a bit of thought to this bomb business?"

"Yes."

"We'll be in touch with you again." He fished in an inner pocket and produced a card. "If you should want me, though, you can find me at this number."

"O.K."

He made a wry face. "I know how you must feel about us."

"Never mind," I said. "Never mind."

Chapter Eight

For most of that week, I flew where I was told to, and thought about radio bombs, and sat on my own in the caravan in the evenings.

Honey didn't come back, but on the day after her visit I had returned from Rotterdam to find a large bag of groceries on the table: eggs, butter, bread, tomatoes, sugar, cheese, powdered milk, tins of soup. Also a pack of six half pints of beer. Also a note from Honey: "Pay me next week."

Not a bad guy, Honey Harley. I took up eating again. Old habits die hard.

Tuesday I took Colin and four assorted others to Wolverhampton races; Wednesday, after the Board of Trade departed, I took a politician to Cardiff to a union strike meeting; and Thursday I took the race-horse trainer to various places in Yorkshire and Northumberland to look at some horses to see if he wanted to buy any.

Thursday evening I made myself a cheese-and-tomato sandwich and a cup of coffee, and ate them looking at the pin-ups, which were curling a bit round the edges. After I'd finished the sandwich, I unstuck the tape and took all the bosomy ladies down. The thrusting pairs of heavily ringed nipples regarded me sorrowfully, like spaniels' eyes. Smiling, I folded them decently over and dropped them in the rubbish bin. The caravan looked just as dingy, however, without them.

Friday morning, when I was in Harley's office filing flight records, Colin rang Harley and said he wanted me to stay overnight at Cambridge, ready again for Saturday.

Harley agreed. "I'll charge Matt's hotel bill to your account."

Colin said, "Fine. But he can stay with me again if he likes."

Harley relayed the message. Did I like? I liked.

Harley put down the receiver. "Trying to save money," he said disparagingly, "having to stay." He brightened: "I'll charge him the hangarage, though."

I took the Cherokee over to Cambridge and fixed for them to give it shelter that night. When Colin came, he was with four other jockeys: three I didn't know, and Kenny Bayst. Kenny said how was I. I was fine, how was he? Good as new, been riding since Newbury, he said.

Between them they had worked out the day's shuttle. All to Brighton, Colin to White Waltham for Windsor, airplane to return to Brighton, pick up the others, return to White Waltham for Colin, return to Cambridge.

"Is that all right?" Colin asked.

"Sure. Anything you say."

He laughed. "The fusses we used to have when we used to ask this sort of thing. . . ."

"Don't see why," I said.

"Larry was a lazy sod. . . ."

They loaded themselves on board and we tracked down east of the London control zone and over the top of Gatwick to Shoreham Airport for Brighton. When we landed, Colin looked at his watch and Kenny nodded and said, "Yeah, he's always faster than Larry. I've noticed it, too."

"Harley will give him the sack," Colin said dryly, unfastening his seat belt.

"He won't, will he?" Kenny sounded faintly anxious. Quicker journeys meant smaller bills.

"It depends on how many customers he pinches

100

from Polyplanes through being fast." Colin grinned at me. "Am I right?"

"Could be," I said.

They went off laughing about it to the waiting taxi. A couple of hours later, Colin came back at a run in his breeches and colors and I whisked him over to White Waltham. He had won, it appeared, at Brighton. A close finish. He was still short of breath. A fast car drove right up to the aircraft as soon as I stopped and had him off down the road to Windsor in a cloud of dust. I went more leisurely back to Shoreham and collected the others at the end of their program. It was a hot sunny day, blue and hazy. They came back sweating.

Kenny had ridden a winner and had brought me a bottle of whisky as a present. I said he didn't need to give me a present.

"Look, sport, if it weren't for you, I wouldn't be riding any more bleeding winners. So take it."

"All right," I said. "Thanks."

"Thanks yourself."

They were tired and expansive. I landed at White Waltham before Colin arrived back from Windsor, and the other four yawned and gossiped, opening all the door and fanning themselves.

". . . gave him a breather coming up the hill."

"That was no breather. That was the soft bugger dropping his bit. Had to give him a sharp reminder to get him going again."

"Can't stand that fellow Fossel. . . ."

"Why do you ride for him, then?"

"Got no choice, have I? Small matter of a retainer. . . ."

". . . What chance you got on Candlestick?"

"Wouldn't finish in the first three if it started now. . . ."

"Hey," said Kenny Bayst, leaning forward and tapping me on the shoulder. "Got something that might interest you, sport." He pulled a sheet of paper out of his trouser pocket. "How about this, then?"

I took the paper and looked at it. It was a leaflet,

high-quality printing on good glossy paper. An invitation to all racegoers to join the Racegoers' Accident Fund.

"I'm not a racegoer," I said.

"No, read it. Go on," he urged. "It came in the post this morning. I thought you'd be interested, so I brought it."

I read down the page: "Up to one thousand pounds for serious personal injury, five thousand pounds for accidental death. Premium five pounds. Double the premium, double the insurance. The insurance everyone can afford. Stable lads, buy security for your missus. Jockeys: out of work but in the money. Race crowds, protect yourself against road accidents on the way home. Trainers who fly to meetings, protect yourself against bombs!"

"Damn it," I said.

Kenny laughed. "I thought you'd like it."

I handed the leaflet, smiling. "Yeah. The so-and-sos."

"Might not be a bad idea, at that."

Colin's hired car drove up and decanted the usual spent force. He climbed wearily into his seat, clipped shut his belt, and said, "Wake me at Cambridge."

"How did it go?" Kenny asked.

"Got that sod Export home by a whisker. . . . But, as for Uptight," he said, yawning, "they might as well send him to the knackers. Got the slows right and proper, that one has."

We woke him at Cambridge. It was a case of waking most of them, in point of fact. They stretched their way onto the tarmac, shirt necks open, ties hanging loose, jackets on their arms. Colin had no jacket, no tie: for him, the customary jeans, the rumpled sweat shirt, the air of being nobody, of being one in a crowd, instead of a crowd in one.

Nancy and Midge had come in the Aston Martin to pick us up. "We brought a picnic," Nancy said, "as it's such a super evening. We're going to that place by the river."

They had also brought swimming trunks for Colin

and a pair of his for me. Nancy swam with us, but Midge said it was too cold. She sat on the bank wearing four watches on her left arm and stretching her long bare legs in the sun.

It was cool and quiet and peaceful in the river after the hot sticky day. The noise of engine throb inside my head calmed to silence. I watched a moorhen gliding along by the reeds, twisting her neck cautiously to fasten me with a shiny eye, peering suspiciously at Colin and Nancy floating a way ahead. I pushed a ripple toward her with my arm. She rode on it like a cork. Simple being a moorhen, I thought. But it wasn't really. All of nature had its pecking order. Everywhere, someone was the pecked.

Nancy and Colin swam back. Friendly eyes, smiling faces. Don't get involved, I thought. Not with anyone. Not yet.

The girls had brought cold chicken and long crisp Cos lettuce leaves with a tangy sauce to dip them in. We ate while the sun went down, and drank a cold bottle of Chablis, sitting on a large blue rug by the river.

When she had finished, Midge lay back on the rug and shielded her eyes from the last slanting rays.

"I wish this could go on forever," she said casually. "The summer, I mean. Warm evenings. We get so few of them."

"We could go and live in the South of France, if you like," Nancy said.

"Don't be silly. . . . Who would look after Colin?"

They smiled, all three of them. The unspoken things were all there. Tragic. Unimportant.

The slow dusk drained all colors into shades of gray. We lazed there, relaxing, chewing stalks of grass, watching the insects flick the surface of the water, talking a little in soft summer-evening murmuring voices.

"We both lost half a stone in Japan, that year we went with Colin. . . ."

"That was the food more than the heat."

"I never did get to like the food. . . ."

"Have you ever been to Japan, Matt?"

"Used to fly there for B.O.A.C."

"B.O.A.C?" Colin was surprised. "Why ever did you leave?"

"Left to please my wife. Long time ago now, though."

"Explains how you fly."

"Oh, sure. . . ."

"I like America better," Midge said. "Do you remember Mr. Kroop, in Laurel, where you got those riding boots made in a day?"

"Mmm. . . ."

"And we kept driving round that shopping center there, and getting lost in the one-way streets. . . ."

"Super, that week was. . . ."

"Wish we could go again. . . ."

There was a long regretful silence. Nancy sat up with a jerk and slapped her leg.

"Bloody mosquitoes."

Colin scratched lazily and nodded. "Time to go home."

We wedged back into the Aston Martin. Colin drove. The twins sat on my legs, leaned on my chest, and twined their arms behind my neck for balance. Not bad, not bad at all. They laughed at my expression.

"Too much of a good thing," Nancy said.

When we went to bed, they both kissed me good night, with identical soft lips, on the cheek.

Breakfast was brisk, businesslike, and accompanied throughout by telephone calls. Annie Villars rang to ask if there was still a spare seat on the Cherokee.

"Who for?" Colin asked cautiously. He made a face at us. "Bloody Fenella," he whispered over the mouthpiece. "No, Annie, I'm terribly sorry. I've promised Nancy. . . ."

"You have?" Nancy said. "First I've heard of it."

He put the receiver down. "I rescue you from Chanter, now it's your turn."

104

"Rescue my foot. You're in and out of the weighing room all day. Fat lot of good that is."

"Do you want to come?"

"Take Midge," she said. "It's her turn."

"No, you go," Midge said. "Honestly, I find it tiring. Especially as it's one of those rush-from-course-to-course days. I'll go along to the meeting here next week. That will do me fine."

"Will you be all right?"

"Naturally I will. I'll lie in the sun in the garden and think of you all exhausting yourselves racing round in circles."

When it turned out that there were two other empty seats as well, in spite of Nancy being there, Annie Villars gave Colin a reproachful look of carefully repressed annoyance and said it would have been useful to have had Fenella along to share the cost. Why else did Colin think she had suggested it?

"I must have miscounted," said Colin happily. "Too late to get her now."

We flew to Bath without incident, Nancy sitting in the righthand seat beside me and acting as co-pilot. It was clear that she intensely enjoyed it, and there was no pain in it for me either. I could see what Larry had meant about practicing short landings, as the Bath runways were incredibly short, but we got down in fair order and parked alongside the opposition's Cessna.

Colin said, "Lock the airplane and come into the races. You can't forever stand on guard."

The Polyplane pilot was nowhere to be seen. I hoped for the best, locked up, and walked with the others in to the racecourse next door.

The first person we saw was Acey Jones, balancing on his crutches with the sun making his pale head look fairer than ever.

"Oh, yes. Colin," Nancy said. "Do you want me to send a fiver to the accident-insurance people? You remember, the leaflet that came yesterday? That man reminded me. . . . He got a thousand pounds from the fund from cracking his ankle. I heard him saying so, at Haydock."

"If you like," he agreed. "A fiver won't break the bank. May as well."

"Bobbie Wessex is sponsoring it," Annie commented.

"Yes." Nancy nodded. "It was on the leaflet."

"Did you see the bit about the bombs?" I asked.

Annie and Nancy both laughed. "Someone in insurance has got a sense of humor, after all."

Annie hustled off to the weighing room to see to her runner in the first race, and Colin followed her to change.

"Lemonade?" I suggested to Nancy.

"Pints of it. Whew, it's hot."

We drank it in a patch of shade, out on the grass. Ten yards away, loud and clear, Eric Goldenberg was conducting a row with Kenny Bayst.

". . . And don't you think, sport, that you can set your gorillas on me and expect me to do your favors afterward, because if you think that, you've got another think coming."

"What gorillas?" Goldenberg demanded, not very convincingly.

"Oh, come off it. Set them to cripple me. At Redcar."

"Must have been those bookmakers you swindled while you were busy double-crossing us."

"I never double-crossed you."

"Don't give me that crap," Goldenberg said heavily. "You know bloody well you did. You twisty little bastard."

"If you think that, why the frigging hell are you asking me to set up another touch for you now?"

"Bygones are bygones."

"Bygones bloody aren't." Kenny spat on the ground at Goldenberg's feet and removed himself to the weighing room. Goldenberg watched him go with narrowed eyes and a venomous twist to his mouth. The next time I saw him, he was holding a well-filled glass and adding substantially to his paunch, while muttering belligerently to a pasty slob who housed all his brains in his biceps. The slob wasn't one of the two who had lammed into Kenny at Redcar. I wondered if Goldenberg intended mustering reinforcements.

"What do you think of Kenny Bayst?" I asked Nancy.

"The big little Mister I-Am from Down Under," she said. "He's better than he used to be, though. He came over here thinking everyone owed him a living, as he'd had a great big successful apprenticeship back home."

"Would he lose to order?"

"I expect so."

"Would he agree to lose to order, take the money, back himself, and try to win?"

She grinned. "You're learning fast."

We watched Colin win the first race. Annie Villars' horse finished third from last. She stood glumly looking at its heaving sides while Kenny's successor made the best of explaining away his own poor showing.

"Annie should have kept Kenny Bayst," Nancy said.

"He wanted out."

"Like Colin doesn't want in." She nodded. "Annie's being a bit of a fool this season."

Before the third race, we went back to the airplane. The Polyplane pilot was standing beside it, peering in through the windows. He was not the stand-off merchant from Redcar, but his colleague from Haydock.

"Good afternoon," Nancy said.

"Good afternoon, Miss Ross." He was polite in the way that is more insolent than rudeness. Not the best method, I would have thought, of seducing Colin's custom back from Derrydowns. He walked away, back to his Cessna, and I went over the Cherokee inch by inch looking for anything wrong. As far as I could see, there was nothing. Nancy and I climbed aboard, and I started the engine to warm it up ready to take off.

Colin and Annie arrived in a hurry and loaded themselves in, and we whisked off across southern England to Shoreham. Colin and Annie again jumped into a waiting taxi and vanished. Nancy stayed with me and the Cherokee, and we sat on the warm grass and watched little airplanes landing and taking off, and talked now and then without pressure about flying, racing, life in general.

Toward the end of the afternoon, she asked, "Will you go on being a taxi pilot all your life?"

"I don't know. I don't look far ahead any more."

"Nor do I," she said.

"No."

"We've been happy, these last few weeks, with Midge being so much better. I wish it would last."

"You'll remember it."

"That's not the same."

"It's only special because of what's coming," I said.

There was a long pause while she thought about it. At length, she asked disbelievingly, "Do you mean that it is because Midge is dying that we are so happy now?"

"Something like that."

She turned her head; considered me. "Tell me something else. I need something else."

"Comfort?"

"If you like."

I said, "You've all three been through the classic progression these last two years. All together, not just Midge herself. Shock, disbelief, anger, and in the end acceptance." I paused. "You've come through the dark tunnel. You're out in the sun the other end. You've done most of your grieving already. You are a most extraordinarily strong family. You'll remember this summer because it will be something worth remembering."

"Matt...."

There were tears in her eyes. I watched the bright little dragonfly airplanes dart and go. They could heal me, the Ross family, I thought. Their strength could heal me. If it would take nothing away from them. If I could be sure.

"What was Colin's wife like?" I asked after a while.

"Oh. . . ." She gave a laugh which was half a sniff. "A bit too much like Fenella. He was much younger then. He didn't know how to duck. She was thirty-three and bossy and rich, and he was twenty and madly impressed by her. To be honest, Midge and I thought she was fabulous, too. We were seventeen and still wet behind the ears. She thought it would be marvelous being married to a genius, all accolades and champagne and glamour. She didn't like it when it turned out to be mostly hard work and starvation and exhaustion. . . . So she left him for a young actor who'd just had rave notices for his first film, and it took Colin months to get back to being himself from the wreck she'd made of him."

"Poor Colin." Or lucky Colin. Strong Colin. Months . . . it was taking me years.

"Yeah." She grinned. "He got over it. He's got some bird now in London. He slides down to see her every so often when he thinks Midge and I aren't noticing."

"I must get me a bird," I said idly. "One of these days."

"You haven't got one?"

I shook my head. I looked at her. Straight eyebrows, straight eyes, sensible mouth. She looked back. I wanted to kiss her. I didn't think she would be angry.

"No," I said absent-mindedly. "No bird."

Take nothing away from them. Nothing from Midge.

"I'll wait a while longer," I said.

Several days—several flights—later, I telephoned the Board of Trade. Diffidently. Sneering at myself for trying to do their job for them, for thinking I might have thought of something they hadn't worked out for themselves. But then I'd been on the flight with the bomb, and they hadn't. I'd seen things, heard things, felt things that they hadn't.

Partly for my own sake, but mainly because of what Nancy had said about the bomb merchant still running around loose with his motives still rotting away inside him, I had finally found myself discarding the thought that it was none of my business, that someone else could sort it all out, and coming round to the view that if I could in fact come up with anything it might be a profitable idea.

To which end I wasted a lot of brain time chasing down labyrinths of speculation, and fetched up against a series of reasons why not.

There was Larry, for instance. Well, what about Larry? Larry had had every chance to put the bomb on board, right up to two hours before I set off to collect the passengers from White Waltham. But however strong a motive he had to kill Colin or ruin Derrydowns—and none had so far appeared bar a few trivial frauds—if it was true it was a radio and not a time bomb, he couldn't have set it off, because when it exploded he was in Turkey. If it had been Larry, a time bomb would have been the only simple and practical way.

Then, Susan. . . . Ridiculous as I thought it, I went over again what the Board of Trade man said: she was going out occasionally with a demolitions expert. Well, good luck to her. The sooner she got married again, the better off I'd be. Only trouble was, the aversion therapy of that last destructive six months seemed to have been just as successful with her as it had been with me.

I couldn't believe that any executive type in his right mind would bump off his occasional girl friend's ex-husband for the sake of about six thousand pounds of insurance, especially as the longer I lived, the greater would be the sum she eventually collected. I had three years ago stopped paying any more premiums, but the value of the payoff automatically went on increasing.

Apart from knowing her incapable of the cold-

blooded murder of innocent people, I respected her
mercenary instincts. The longer I lived, the better off
she would be on all counts. It was as simple as that.

Honey Harley . . . had said she would do "anything"
to keep Derrydowns in business, and the blowing up
of the Cherokee had eased the financial situation.
One couldn't sell things which were being bought on
the hire-purchase, and if one couldn't keep up the
installments the aircraft technically belonged to the
H.P. company, who might sell it at a figure which did
little more than cover themselves, leaving a molehill
for Derrydowns to salvage. Insurance, on the other
hand, had done them proud: paid off the H.P. and left
them with capital in hand.

Yet killing Colin Ross would have ruined Derrydowns completely. Honey Harley would never have
killed any of the customers, let alone Colin Ross. And
the same applied to Harley himself, all along the line.

The Polyplane people, then? Always around, always belligerent, trying their damnedest to put Derrydowns out of business and win back Colin Ross.
Well . . . the bomb would have achieved the first
object but have put the absolute dampers on the
second. I couldn't see even the craziest Polyplane
pilot killing the golden goose.

Kenny Bayst . . . livid with Eric Goldenberg, Major
Tyderman, and Annie Villars. But, as I'd said to
Colin, where would he have got a bomb from in the
time, and would he have killed Colin and me, too? It
didn't seem possible, any of it. No to Kenny Bayst.

Who, then?

Who?

Since I couldn't come up with anyone else, I went
back over the possibilities all over again. Larry, Susan,
the Harleys, Polyplanes, Kenny Bayst. Looked at them
up, down, and sideways. Got nowhere. Made some
coffee, went to bed, went to sleep.

Woke up at four in the morning with the moon
shining on my face. And one fact hitting with a bang.
Look at things laterally. Start from the bottom.

I started from the bottom. When I did that, the

answer rose up and stared me in the face. I couldn't believe it. It was too darned simple.

In the morning, I made a lengthy telephone call to a long-lost cousin, and two hours later got one back. And it was then, expecting a flat rebuff, that I rang up the Board of Trade.

The tall polite man wasn't in. He would, they said, call back later.

When he did, Harley was airborne with a pupil and Honey answered in the tower. She buzzed through to the crew room, where I was writing up records.

"The Board of Trade want you. What have you been up to?"

"It's only that old bomb," I said soothingly.

"Huh."

When the tall man came on the line, she was still listening on the tower extension.

"Honey," I said. "Quit."

"I beg your pardon," said the Board of Trade.

Honey giggled, but she put her receiver down. I heard the click.

"Captain Shore?" the voice said reprovingly.

"Er, yes."

"You wanted me?"

"You said . . . if I thought of any angle on the bomb."

"Indeed, yes." A shade of warmth.

"I've been thinking," I said, "about the transmitter which was needed to set it off."

"Yes?"

"How big would the bomb have been?" I asked. "All that plastic explosive and gunpowder and wires and solenoids?"

"I should think quite small. . . . You would probably pack a bomb like that into a flat tin about seven inches by four by two inches deep. Possibly even smaller. The tighter they are packed, the more fiercely they explode."

"And how big would the transmitter have to be to send perhaps three different signals?"

"Nowadays, not very big. If size were important . . .

112

a pack of cards, perhaps. But in this case I would have thought . . . larger. The transmissions must have had to carry a fairly long way . . . and to double the range of a signal you have to quadruple the power of the transmitter, as no doubt you know."

"Yes. . . . I apologize for going through all this the long way, but I wanted to be sure. Because although I don't know *why*, I've got a good idea of *when* and *who*."

"What did you say?" His voice sounded strangled.

"I said—"

"Yes, yes," he interrupted. "I heard. When—when, then?"

"It was put on board at White Waltham. Taken off at Haydock. And put back on again at Haydock."

"What do you mean?"

"It came with one of the passengers."

"Which one?"

"By the way," I said. "How much would such a bomb cost?"

"Oh—about eighty pounds or so," he said impatiently. "Who?"

"And would it take a considerable expert to make one?"

"Someone used to handling explosives and with a working knowledge of radio."

"I thought so."

"Look," he said, "look, will you please stop playing cat-and-mouse. I dare say it amuses you to tease the Board of Trade. . . . I don't say I absolutely blame you, but will you please plainly tell me which of the passengers had a bomb with him?"

"Major Tyderman," I said.

"Major . . ." He took an audible breath. "Are you meaning to say now that it wasn't the bomb rolling around on the elevator wires that caused the friction which persuaded you to land? . . . That Major Tyderman was carrying it around unknown to himself all the afternoon? Or what?"

"No," I said. "And no."

"For God's sake. . . ." He was exasperated. "I sup-

113

pose you couldn't simplify the whole thing by telling me exactly who planted the bomb on Major Tyderman? Who intended to blow him up?"

"If you like."

He took a shaking grip. I smiled at the crew-room wall.

"Well, who?"

"Major Tyderman," I said. "Himself."

Silence. Then a protest.

"Do you mean suicide? It can't have been. The bomb went off when the airplane was on the ground. . . ."

"Precisely," I said.

"What?"

"If a bomb goes off in an airplane, everyone automatically thinks that it was intended to blow up in the air and kill all the people on board."

"Yes, of course."

"Suppose the real intended victim was the airplane itself, not the people?"

"But why?"

"I told you, I don't know why."

"All right," he said. "All right." He took a deep breath. "Let's start from the beginning. You are saying that Major Tyderman, intending to blow up the airplane for reasons unknown, took a bomb with him to the races."

"Yes."

"What makes you think so?"

"Looking back. . . . He was rigidly tense all day, and he wouldn't be parted from his binocular case, which was large enough to contain a bomb of the size you described."

"That's absurdly circumstantial," he protested.

"Sure," I agreed. "Then, it was the Major who borrowed the keys from me to go over to the aircraft to fetch the *Sporting Life* which he had left there. He wouldn't let me go, though I offered. He came back and gave me the keys. Of course, he hadn't locked up. He wanted to create a little confusion. While he was over there, he unscrewed the back panel of the luggage bay and put the bomb behind it, against the fuselage. Limpet gadget, I expect, as I said before, which came unstuck on the bumpy flight."

"He couldn't have foreseen you'd land in East Midlands. . . ."

"It didn't matter where we landed. As soon as everyone was clear of the aircraft, he was ready to blow it up."

"That's sheer guesswork."

"He did it in front of my eyes, at East Midlands. I saw him look round, to check there was no one near it. Then he was fiddling with his binocular case— sending the signals. They could have been either very low or super-high frequencies. They didn't have very far to go. But, more important, the transmitter would have been very low-powered . . . and very small."

"But—by all accounts—and yours, too—he was severely shocked after the explosion."

"Shocked by the sight of the disintegration he had been sitting on all day. And acting a bit, too."

He thought it over at length. Then he said, "Wouldn't someone have noticed that the Major wasn't using binoculars although he was carrying the case?"

"He could say he'd just dropped them and they were broken . . . and anyway he carries a flask in that case normally as well as the race glasses. . . . Lots of people must have seen him taking a swig, as I have. They wouldn't think it odd. They might think he'd brought the flask but forgotten the glasses."

I could imagine him shaking his head. "It's a fantastic theory altogether. And not a shred of evidence. Just a guess." He paused. "I'm sorry, Mr. Shore, I'm certain you've done your best, but . . ."

I noticed he'd demoted me from captain. I smiled thinly.

"There's one other tiny thing," I said gently.

"Yes?" He was slightly, very slightly apprehensive, as if expecting yet more fantasy.

"I got in touch with a cousin in the army and he

115

looked up some old records for me. In World War II, Major Tyderman was in the Royal Engineers, in charge of a unit which spent nearly all of its time in England."

"I don't see—"

"They were dealing," I said, "with unexploded bombs."

Chapter Nine

It was next day that Nancy flew Colin to Haydock. They went in the four-seat 140-horsepower small-version Cherokee, which she normally hired from her flying club for lessons and practice, and they set off from Cambridge shortly before I left there myself with a full load in the replacement Six. I had been through her flight plan with her and helped her all I could with the many technicalities and regulations she would meet in the complex Manchester control zone. The weather forecast was for clear skies until evening; there would be radar to help her if she got lost; and I would be listening to her nearly all the time on the radio as I followed her up.

Colin grinned at me. "Harley would be horrified at the care you're taking to look after her. 'Let them frighten themselves silly,' he'd say. 'Then he'll fly with us all the time, with none of this do-it-yourself nonsense.'"

"Yeah," I said. "And Harley wants you safe, too, don't forget."

"Did he tell you to help us?"

"Not actually, no."

"Thought not."

Harley had said crossly, "I don't want them making a habit of it. Persuade Colin Ross she isn't experienced enough."

Colin didn't need persuading: he knew. He also

117

wanted to please Nancy. She set off with shining eyes, like a child being given a treat.

The Derrydowns Six had been hired by an un-clued-up trainer who had separately agreed to share the trip with both Annie Villars and Kenny Bayst. Even diluted by the hiring trainer, the large loud-voiced owner of the horse he was running, and the jockey who was to ride it, the atmosphere at loading time was poisonous.

Jarvis Kitch, the hiring trainer, who could have helped, retreated into a huff.

"How was I to know," he complained to me in aggrieved anger, "that they loathe each other's guts?"

"You couldn't," I said soothingly.

"They just rang up and asked if there was a spare seat. Annie yesterday, Bayst the day before. I said there was. How was I to know?"

"You couldn't."

The loud-voiced owner, who was evidently footing the bill, asked testily what the hell it mattered, they would be contributing their share of the cost. He had a North Country accent and a bullying manner, and he was the sort of man who considered that when he bought a man's services he bought his soul. Kitch subsided hastily: the small attendant jockey remained cowed and silent throughout. The owner, whose name I later discovered from the race card was Ambrose, then told me to get a move on as he hadn't hired me to stand around all day on the ground at Cambridge.

Annie Villars suggested in embarrassment that the captain of an aircraft was like the captain of a ship.

"Nonsense," he said. "In a two-bit little outfit like this, he's only a chauffeur. Taking me from place to place, isn't he? For hire?" He nodded. "Chauffeur." His voice left no one in any doubt about his opinion on the proper place of chauffeurs.

I sighed, climbed aboard, strapped myself in. Easy to ignore him, as it was far from the first time in my life I'd met that attitude. All the same, hardly one of the jolliest of trips.

The Cherokee Six cruised at fifty miles an hour
118

faster than the 140, so that I passed Nancy some-where on the way up. I could hear her calling the various flight-information regions on the radio, as she could hear me. It was companionable, in an odd sort of way. And she was doing all right.

I landed at Haydock a few minutes before her, and unloaded the passengers in time to watch her come in. She put on a show to impress the audience, touching down like a feather on the grass. I grinned to myself. Not bad for a ninety-five-hour amateur. It hadn't been the easiest of trips, either. There would be no holding her after this.

She rolled to a stop a little way along the rails from me, and I finished locking the Six and walked over to tell her she would smash the undercarriage next time she thumped an airplane down like that.

She made a face at me, excited and pleased. "It was super. Great. The Liverpool radar people were awfully kind. They told me exactly which headings to fly round the control zone, and then told me they would put me smack overhead the racecourse, and they did."

Colin was proud of her and teased her affectionate-ly. "Sure, we've got here, but we've got to go home yet."

"Going home's always easier," she said confidently. "And there are none of those difficult control-zone rules round Cambridge."

We walked together across the track to the pad-dock, ducking under the rails. Nancy talked the whole way, as high as if she'd taken Benzedrine. Colin grinned at me. I grinned back. Nothing as intoxicating as a considerable achievement.

We left him at the weighing room and went off to have some coffee.

"Do you know it's only four weeks since we were at Haydock before?" she said. "Since the bomb. Only four weeks. I seem to have known you half my life."

"I hope you'll know me for the other half," I said.

"What did you say?"

"Nothing . . . Turkey sandwiches all right?"

"Mmm, lovely." She looked at me, unsure. "What did you mean?"

"Just one of those pointless things people say."

"Oh."

She bit into the soft thick sandwich. She had good straight teeth. I was being a fool, I thought. A fool to get involved, a fool to grow fond of her. I had nothing but a lot of ruins to offer anyone, and she had the whole world to choose from, the sister of Colin Ross. If I was an iceberg, as Honey said, I'd better stay an iceberg. When ice melted, it made a mess.

"You've clammed up," she said, observing me.

"I haven't."

"Oh, yes, you have. You do, sometimes. You look relaxed and peaceful, and then something inside goes snap shut and you retreat out into the stratosphere. Somewhere very cold." She shivered. "Freezing."

I drank my coffee and let the stratosphere do its stuff. The melting edges safely refroze.

"Will Chanter be here today?" I asked.

"God knows." She shrugged. "Do you want him to be?"

"No." It sounded more vehement than I meant.

"That's something, anyhow," she said under her breath.

I let it go. She couldn't mean what it sounded like. We finished the sandwiches and went out to watch Colin ride, and after that, while we were leaning against the parade-ring rails, Chanter appeared out of nowhere and smothered Nancy in hair and fringes and swirling fabric, as closely as if he were putting out a fire with a carpet.

She pushed him away. "For God's sake . . ."

He was unabashed. "Aw, Nancy. C'mon now. You and me, we'd have everything going for us if you'd just loosen up."

"You're a bad trip, Chanter, as far as I'm concerned."

"You've never been on any real trip, chick, that's your problem."

"And I'm not going," she said firmly.

120

"A little acid lets you into the guts of things."

"Components," I said. "As you said before. You see things in fragments."

"Huh?" Chanter focused on me. "Nancy, you still got this creep in tow? You must be joking."

"He sees things whole," she said. "No props needed."

"Acid isn't a prop, it's a doorway," he declaimed.

"Shut the door," she said. "I'm not going through."

Chanter scowled at me. The green chenille tablecloth had been exchanged for a weird shapeless tunic made of irregular-shaped pieces of fabrics, fur, leather, and metal, all stapled together instead of sewn.

"This is your doing, man, you're bad news."

"It's not his doing," Nancy said. "The drug scene is a drag. It always was. Maybe at art school I thought getting woozy on pot was a gas, but not any more. I've grown up, Chanter. I've told you before, I've grown up."

"He's brainwashed you."

She shook her head. I knew she was thinking of Midge. Face something big enough and you always grow up.

"Don't you have any classes today?" she asked.

He scowled more fiercely. "The sods are out on strike."

She laughed. "Do you mean the students?"

"Yeah. Demanding the sack for the deputy Head for keeping a record of what demos they go to."

I asked ironically, "Which side are you on?"

He peered at me. "You bug me, man, you do really."

For all that, he stayed with us all afternoon, muttering, scowling, plonking his hands on Nancy whenever he got the chance. Nancy bore his company as if she didn't altogether dislike it. As for me, I could have done without it. Easily.

Colin won two races, including the day's biggest. Annie Villars' horse came second, Kenny Bayst won a race on an objection. The loud-voiced Ambrose's horse finished fast but fourth, which didn't bode well for sweetness and light on the way home.

The way home was beginning to give me faint twinges of speculation. The weak warm front which had been forecast for late evening looked as if it were arriving well before schedule. From the southwest, the upper winds were drawing a strip of cloud over the sky like a sheet over a bed.

Nancy looked up when the sun went in.

"Golly, where did all that cloud come from?"

"It's the warm front."

"Damn. . . . Do you think it will have got to Cambridge?"

"I'll find out for you, if you like."

I telephoned to Cambridge and asked them for their actual and forecast weather. Nancy stood beside me inside the telephone box, and Chanter fumed suspiciously outside. I had to ask Cambridge to repeat what they'd said. Nancy smelled faintly of a fresh flowering scent. "Did you say two thousand feet?" Yes, said Cambridge with exaggerated patience, we've told you twice already.

I put down the receiver. "The front isn't expected there for three or four hours, and the forecast cloud base even then is as high as two thousand feet, so you should be all right."

"Anyway," she said, "I've done dozens of practice letdowns with Cambridge. Even if it should be cloudy by the time we get back, I'm sure I could do it in earnest."

"Have you ever done it without an instructor?"

She nodded. "Several times. On fine days, of course."

I pondered. "You aren't legally qualified yet to carry passengers in clouds."

"Don't look so fraught. I won't have to. They said it was clear there now, didn't they? And if the base is two thousand feet when I get there, I can keep below that easily."

"Yes, I suppose you can."

"And I've got to get back, haven't I?" she said reasonably.

122

"Mmm. . . ."

Chanter pulled open the telephone-box door. "You taking a lease on that space, man?" he inquired. He put his arm forward over Nancy's chest a millimeter south of her breasts and scooped her out. She half disappeared into the enveloping fuzz and emerged blushing.

"Chanter, for God's sake, we're at the races!"

"Transfer to my pad, then."

"No, thank you."

"Women," he said in disgust. "Goddamn women. Don't know what's good for them."

"How's that for a right-wing reactionary statement?" I inquired of the air in general.

"You cool it, man. Just cool it."

Nancy smoothed herself down and said, "Both of you cool it. I'm going back to the airplane now to get set for going home, and you're not coming with me, Chanter. I can't concentrate with you crawling all over me."

He stayed behind with bad grace, complaining bitterly when she took me with her.

"He's impossible," she said as we walked across the track. But she was smiling.

Spreading the map out on the wing, I went through the flight plan with her, step by step, as that was what she wanted. She was going back as we'd come, via the radio beacon at Lichfield: not a straight line but the easiest way to navigate. As she had said, it was a simpler business going home. I worked out the times between points for her and filled them in on her planning sheet.

"You are five times as quick at it as I am." She sighed.

"I've had a spot more practice."

I folded the map and clipped the completed plan onto it. "See you at Cambridge," I said. "With a bit of luck."

"Meany."

"Nancy. . . ."

"Yes?"

I didn't exactly know what I wanted to say. She waited. After a while, I said earnestly, "Take care."

She half smiled. "I will, you know."

Colin came across the track, dragging his feet. "God, I'm tired," he said. "How's my pilot?"

"Ready, willing, and, if it's your lucky day, able."

I did the external checks for her while they climbed aboard. No bombs to be seen. Didn't expect any. She started the engine after I'd given her the all clear, and they both waved as she taxied off. She turned into wind at the far end of the field, accelerated quickly, and lifted off into the pale gray sky. The clouds were a shade lower than they had been. Nothing to worry about. Not if it was clear at Cambridge.

I strolled across to the Derrydowns Six. Annie Villars and Kenny Bayst were both there already, studiously looking in opposite directions. I unlocked the doors, and Annie embarked without a word. Kenny gave her a sour look and stayed outside on the ground. I congratulated him on his winner. It all helped, he said.

Ambrose's trainer and jockey trickled back looking pensive, and finally Ambrose came himself, reddish in the face and breathing out beer fumes in a sickly cloud. As soon as he reached the aircraft, he leaned toward me and gave me the full benefit.

"I've left me hat in the cloakroom," he said. "Hop over and fetch it for me."

Kenny and the other two were all of a sudden very busy piling themselves aboard and pretending they hadn't heard. Short of saying "Fetch it yourself" and losing Harley a customer, I was stuck with it. I trudged back across the track, through the paddock, into the members' Gents, and collected the hat off the peg it was hanging on. Its band was so greasy that I wondered how Ambrose had the nerve to let anyone see it.

Turned, made for the door. Felt my arm clutched in a fiercely urgent grip.

I swung round. The hands holding on to my arm like steel grabs belonged to Major Tyderman.

"Major," I exclaimed in surprise. I hadn't seen him there all through the afternoon.

"Shore!" He was far more surprised to see me. And more than surprised. Horrified. The color was draining out of his face while I watched.

"Shore. . . . What are you doing here? Did you come back?"

Puzzled, I said, "I came over for Mr. Ambrose's hat."

"But—you flew—you took off with Colin and Nancy Ross."

I shook my head. "No, I didn't. Nancy was flying."

"But—you came with them." He sounded agonized.

"I didn't. I flew the Six here with five passengers." The extreme state of his shock got through to me like a tidal wave. He was clinging on to my arm now more for support than to attract my attention.

"Major," I said, the terrible, terrifying suspicion shaking in my voice, "you haven't put another bomb on that aircraft? Not—oh, God—another bomb?"

"I—I—" His voice strangled in his throat.

"Major." I disengaged my arm and seized both of his. Ambrose's hat fell and rolled unnoticed on the dirty floor. "Major." I squeezed him viciously. *"Not another bomb?"*

"No—but—"

"But *what?*"

"I thought—you were flying them— I thought you were with them— You would be able to cope. . . ."

"Major." I shook him, gripping as if I'd pull his arms in two. "What have you done to that airplane?"

"I saw you—come with them, when they came. And go back—and look at the map—and do the checks. . . . I was sure—it was you that was flying— and you—you—could deal with— But Nancy Ross. . . . Oh, my God. . . ."

I let go one of his arms and slapped him hard in the face.

"What have you done to that airplane?"

"You can't—do anything. . . ."

125

"I'll get her back. Get her down on the ground at once."

He shook his head. "You won't—be able to. . . . She'll have no radio. . . . I put . . ." He swallowed and put his hand to his face where I'd hit him. "I put—a plaster—nitric acid—on the lead—to the master switch. . . ."

I let go of his other arm and simply looked at him, feeling the coldness sink in. Then I blindly picked up Ambrose's hat and ran out of the door. Ran. Ran across the paddock, across the track, down to the aircraft. I didn't stop to slap out of the Major what he'd done it for. Didn't think of it. Thought only of Nancy Ross with her limited experience having to deal with a total electrical failure.

She could do it, of course. The engine wouldn't stop. Several of the instruments would go on working. The altimeter, the air-speed indicator, the compass— none of those essentials would be affected. They worked on magnetism, air pressure, and engine-driven gyroscopes, not electricity.

All the engine instruments would read zero, and the fuel gauge would register empty. She wouldn't know how much fuel she had left. But she did know, I thought, that she had enough for at least two hours' flying.

The worst thing was the radio. She would have no communication with the ground, nor could she receive any signals from the navigation beacons. Well . . . dozens of people flew without radio, without even having it installed at all. If she was worried about getting lost, she could land at the first suitable airfield.

It might not have happened yet, I thought. Her radio might still be working. The nitric acid might not yet have eaten through the main electrical cable.

While I was on the ground, I was too low down for them to hear me, but if I got up in the air fast enough, I could tell the Manchester control people the situation, get them to relay the facts to her, tell her to land at an airfield as soon as she could. . . . A fairly simple matter to repair the cable, once she was safe on the ground.

I gave Ambrose his hat. He was still outside on the grass, waiting for me to climb through to the left-hand seat. I shifted myself across onto it with no seconds wasted, and he hauled himself up after me. By the time he'd strapped himself in, I had the engine running, my headset in place, and the radios warming up.

"What's the rush?" Ambrose inquired as we taxied at just under takeoff speed down to the far end.

"Have to send a radio message to Colin Ross, who's in the air ahead of us."

"Oh." He nodded heavily. He knew the Rosses had come up when we had, knew that Nancy was flying. "All right, then."

I thought fleetingly that if he thought I couldn't even hurry without getting his permission first, he was in for a moderate shock. I wasn't taking him back to Cambridge until I was certain Nancy and Colin were safe.

As there was only one headset on board, Ambrose couldn't hear any incoming transmissions, and with the microphone close against my lips I doubted if he could hear over the engine noise anything I sent outward. I thought I would delay as long as possible inviting his objections.

Two hundred feet off the ground, I raised the Air Traffic Controller at Liverpool. Explained that Nancy's radio might be faulty; asked if he had heard her.

Yes, he had. He'd given her radar clearance out of the control zone, and handed her on to Preston Information. Since I had to stay on his frequency until I was out of the zone myself, I asked him to find out from Preston if they still had contact with her.

"Stand by," he said.

After a long two minutes, he came back. "They did have," he said briefly. "They lost her in the middle of one of her transmissions. They can't raise her now."

Sod the Major, I thought violently. Stupid, dangerous little man.

I kept my voice casual. "Did they have her position?"

"Stand by." A pause. He came back. "She was on track to Lichfield, E.T.A. Lichfield five three, flying visual on top at flight level four five."

"On top?" I repeated with apprehension.

"Affirmative."

We had been climbing steadily ourselves. We went into thin cloud at two thousand feet and came through it into the sunshine at four thousand. Everywhere below us in all directions spread the cotton-wool blanket, hiding the earth beneath. She would have had to climb to that height as well, because the Pennines to the east of Manchester rose to nearly three thousand feet and the high ridges would have been sticking up into the clouds. With no room for her between the clouds and the hills, she would have either had to go back or go up. She wouldn't see any harm in going up. With radio navigation and a good forecast for Cambridge, it was merely the sensible thing to do.

"Her destination is Cambridge," I said. "Can you check the weather there?"

"Stand by." A much longer pause. Then his voice, dead level, spelling it out. "Cambridge actual weather, cloud has spread in fast from the southwest, now eight-eighths cover, base twelve hundred feet, tops three thousand five hundred."

I didn't acknowledge him at once: was digesting the appalling implications.

"Confirm weather copied," he said baldly.

"Weather copied."

"Latest meteorological reports indicate total cloud cover over the entire area south of the Tees." He knew exactly what he was saying. The laconic non-panic voice was deliberately unexcited. Nancy was flying above the cloud layer with no means of telling where she was. She couldn't see the ground and couldn't ask anyone for directions. Eventually she would have to come down, because she would run out of fuel. With the gauge out of action, she couldn't tell exactly how long she could stay airborne, and it was essential for her to go down through the clouds while the engine was still running, so that she could find somewhere to land once she was underneath. But if she went down too soon or in the wrong place, she could all too easily fly into a cloud-covered hill. Even for a highly experienced pilot, it was a sticky situation.

I said, with the same studied artificial calm, "Can the R.A.F. radar stations find her and trace where she goes? I know her flight plan. . . . I made it out for her. She is likely to stick to it, as she thinks it is still clear at Cambridge. I could follow . . . and find her."

"Stand by." Again the pause for consultations. "Change frequency to Birmingham radar on one two three three."

"Roger," I said. "And thanks very much."

"Good luck," he said. "You'll need it."

Chapter Ten

He had explained the situation to Birmingham. I gave the radar controller Nancy's planned track and air speed and estimated time for Lichfield, and after a few moments he came back and said there were at least ten aircraft on his screen which were possibles, but he had no way of telling who they were. "I'll consult with the R.A F. Wymeswold. . . . They may not be as busy as we are. They can concentrate on it more."

"Tell them that at about five three she will change her heading to one two five."

"Roger," he said. "Stand by."

He came back. "R.A.F. Wymeswold say they will watch for her."

"Great," I said.

After a few moments, he said in an incredulous voice, "We have a report that Colin Ross is aboard the non-radio aircraft. Can you confirm?"

"Affirmative" I said. "The pilot is his sister."

"Good God," he said. "Then we'd better find her."

I had got them to route me straight through the control zone instead of round it, and was making for Northwich, and then the Lichfield beacon. We had taken off, I calculated, a good thirty minutes behind her, and in spite of the short cut and the Six's superior speed, it would be barely possible to overtake her before Cambridge. I looked at my watch for about the twentieth time. Five-fifty. At five-fifty-three, she would be turning over Lichfield . . . except that she wouldn't know she was at Lichfield. If she turned as scheduled, it would be on her part simply blind faith.

Birmingham radar called me up. "Cambridge report a steady deterioration in the weather. The cloud base is now eight hundred feet."

"Roger," I said flatly.

After another five minutes, during which five-fifty-three came and went in silence, he said, "Wymeswold report that an aircraft on their screen has turned from one six zero onto one two five, but it is five miles northeast of Lichfield. The aircraft is unidentified. They will maintain surveillance."

"Roger," I said.

She could be drifting northeast, I thought, because the wind from the southwest was stronger than it had been on the northward journey, and I hadn't made enough allowance for it on the flight plan. I pressed the transmit button and informed the radarman.

"I'll tell them," he said.

We flew on. I looked round at the passengers. They looked variously bored, thoughtful, and tired. Probably none of them would notice when we left our direct course to go and look for Nancy: but they'd certainly notice if or when we found her.

"Wymeswold report the aircraft they were watching has turned north onto zero one zero."

"Oh, no," I said.

"Stand by. . . ."

Too easy, I thought despairingly. It had been too easy. The aircraft which had turned onto the right heading at the right time at roughly the right place hadn't been the right aircraft after all. I took three deep deliberate breaths. Concentrated on the fact that wherever she was she was in no immediate danger. She could stay up for more than another hour and a half.

I had over an hour in which to find her. In roughly three thousand square miles of sky as featureless as the desert. Piece of cake.

"Wymeswold report that the first aircraft has apparently landed at East Midlands, but that they have another possibility ten miles east of Lichfield, present heading one two zero. They have no height information."

"Roger," I said again. No height information meant that the blip on their screen could be flying at anything up to thirty thousand feet or more, not four thousand five hundred.

"Stand by."

I stood by. Mentally bit my nails. Slid a sidelong glance at Ambrose and went unhurriedly about checking our own height, speed, direction. Lichfield dead ahead, eleven minutes away. Forty minutes to Cambridge. Too long. Have to go faster. Pushed the throttle open another notch and came up against the stops. Full power. Nothing more to be done.

"Possible aircraft now tracking steady one zero five. Present track if maintained will take it thirty miles north of Cambridge at estimated time two zero."

"Roger." I looked at my watch. Did a brief sum. Pressed the transmit button. "That's the wrong aircraft. It's traveling too fast. At ninety knots, she couldn't reach the Cambridge area before three five or four zero."

"Understood." A short silence. "Retune now to R.A.F. Cottesmore, Northern Radar, one four two decimal two nine. I'm handing you on to them."

I thanked him. Returned. Cottesmore said they were in the picture, and looking. They had seven unidentified aircraft traveling from west to east to the south of them, all at heights unknown.

Seven. She could be any one of them. She could have gone completely haywire and turned round and headed back to Manchester. I felt my skin prickle. Surely she would have enough sense not to fly straight into a control zone without radio. And anyway she still believed it was clear at Cambridge. . . .

I reached the Lichfield beacon. Turned onto course for Cambridge. Informed Cottesmore radar that I had done so. They didn't have me on their screen yet, they said: I was still too far away.

I tracked doggedly on toward Cambridge over the cotton-wool wastes. The sun shone hotly into the cabin, and all the passengers except Ambrose went to sleep.

"One unidentified aircraft has landed at Leicester," Cottesmore radar said. "Another appears to be heading directly for Peterborough."

"That leaves five?" I asked.

"Six. . . . There's another now further to the west."

"It may be me."

"Turn left thirty degrees for identification."

I turned, flew on the new heading.

"Identified," he said. "Return to former heading."

I turned back on track, stifling the raw anxiety which mounted with every minute. They must find her, I thought. They *must.*

Cottesmore said, "One aircraft which passed close to the south of us five minutes ago has now turned north."

Not her.

"The same aircraft has now flown in a complete circle and resumed a track of one one zero."

It might be. If she had spotted a thin patch. Had gone to see if she could see the ground and get down safely to below the cloud. Had found she couldn't: had gone on again in what she thought was the direction of Cambridge.

"That might be her," I said. Or someone else in the same difficulties. Or someone simply practicing turns. Or anything.

"That particular aircraft has now turned due south . . . slightly west . . . now round again to southeast . . . back on one one zero."

"Could be looking for thin patches in the cloud," I said.

"Could be. Stand by." A pause. Then his voice, remote and careful. "Cloud base in this area is down to six hundred feet. Eight-eighths cover. No clear patches."

Oh, Nancy. . . .

"I'm going to look for that one," I said. "Can you give me a steer to close on its present track?"

"Will do," he said. "Turn left onto zero nine five. You are thirty-two miles to the west. I estimate your ground speed at one fifty knots. The aircraft in question is traveling at about ninety-five knots."

In the twelve minutes it would take me to reach the other aircraft's present position, it would have shifted twenty further on. Catching up would take twenty-five to thirty minutes.

"The aircraft in question is circling again . . . now tracking one one zero. . . ."

The more it circled, the sooner I'd catch it. But if it wasn't Nancy after all . . . I thrust the thought violently out of my mind. If it wasn't Nancy, we might never find her.

Ambrose touched my arm, and I had been concentrating so hard that I jumped.

"We're off course," he said dogmatically. He tapped the compass. "We're going due east. We'd better not be lost."

"We're under radar control," I said matter-of-factly.

"Oh. . . ." He was uncertain. "I see."

I would have to tell him, I thought. Couldn't put it off any longer. I explained the situation as briefly as I could, leaving out Major Tyderman's part in it and shouting to make myself heard over the noise of the engine.

He was incredulous. "Do you mean we're chasing all over the sky looking for Colin Ross?"

"Directed by radar," I said briefly.

"And who," he asked belligerently, "is going to pay for this? I am certainly not. In fact, you have been totally irresponsible in changing course without asking my permission first."

Cottesmore reported, "The aircraft is now overhead Stamford, and circling again."

"Roger," I said. And for God's sake, Nancy, I thought, don't try going down through the cloud just there. There were some hills round about a radio mast five hundred feet high.

"Steer one zero zero to close."

"One zero zero."

"Aircraft has resumed its former heading."

I took a considerable breath of relief.

"Did you hear what I said?" Ambrose demanded angrily.

"We have a duty to go to the help of an aircraft in trouble," I said.

"Not at my expense, we don't."

"You will be charged," I said patiently, "only the normal amount for the trip."

"That's not the point. You should have asked my permission. I am seriously displeased. I will complain to Harley. We should not have left our course. Someone else should have gone to help Colin Ross. Why should we be inconvenienced?"

"I am sure he will be pleased to hear your views," I said politely. "And no doubt he will pay any expenses incurred in his rescue."

He glared at me speechlessly, swept by fury.

Annie Villars leaned forward and tapped me on the shoulder.

"Did I hear you say that Colin Ross is lost? Up here, do you mean? On top of the clouds?"

I glanced round. They were all awake, all looking concerned.

"Yes," I said briefly. "With no radio. The radar people think they may have found him. We're going over to see . . . and to help."

"Anything we can do. . . ." Annie said. "Of course, call on us."

I smiled at her over my shoulder. Ambrose turned round to her and started to complain. She shut him up smartly. "Do you seriously propose we make no attempt to help? You must be out of your mind. It is our clear and absolute duty to do whatever we can. And a captain doesn't have to consult his passengers before he goes to another ship in distress."

He said something about expense. Annie said crisply, "If you are too mean to pay a few extra pounds as your share of perhaps saving the life of Colin Ross,

I shall be pleased to contribute the whole amount myself."

"Atta girl," Kenny Bayst said loudly. Annie Villars looked startled, but not displeased. Ambrose swiveled to face forward. He had turned a dark purplish red. I hoped it was shame and embarrassment, not an incipient thrombosis.

"The aircraft is circling again," Cottesmore reported. "Its position now is just south of Peterborough. . . . Remain on your present heading. . . . I am handing you on now to Wytton. . . . No need for you to explain to them . . . they know the situation."

"Thank you very much," I said.

"Good luck. . . ."

Wytton, the next in the chain, the R.A.F. master station northeast of Cambridge, was crisp, cool, efficient.

"Cloud base at Cambridge six hundred feet, no further deterioration in past half hour. Visibility three kilometers in light rain. Surface wind two four zero, ten knots."

"Weather copied," I said automatically. I was looking at the map. Another radio mast, this one seven hundred feet high, south of Peterborough. Go on, Nancy, I thought, go on further east. Don't try there. Not there . . .

Wytton said, "Aircraft now back on one zero."

I rubbed a hand round the back of my neck. I could feel the sweat.

"Steer zero nine five. You are now ten miles west of the aircraft."

"I'm climbing to flight level eight zero. To see better."

"Cleared to eight zero."

The altimeter hands crept round to eight thousand feet. The blanket of white fleece spread out unbroken in all directions to the horizon, soft and pretty in the sun. The passengers murmured, perhaps realizing for the first time the extent of Nancy's predicament. Mile after mile after mile of emptiness, and absolutely no way of telling where she was.

"Aircraft's circling again. . . . Maintain zero nine five. You are now seven miles to the west."

I said over my shoulder to Annie Villars, "We'll see them soon. . . . Would you take this notebook"—I handed her the spiral-bound reporters' notebook I used for jotting during flights—"and make some letters out of the pages? As big as you can. We will need, you see, to hold them up in the window, so that Nancy and Colin can read what we want them to do."

And let it be them, I thought coldly. Just let it be them, and not some other poor lost souls. Because we'd have to stay to help. We couldn't leave them to struggle, and look somewhere else for the ones we wanted. . . .

Annie Villars fumbled in her handbag and produced a small pair of scissors.

"Which letters?" she said economically. "You say, and I'll write them down, and then make them."

"Right. . . . F O L W B A S E. That will do to start with."

I twisted my head and saw her start snipping. She was making the letters full-page size and as bold as possible. Satisfed, I looked forward again, scanning the sunny waste, searching for a small black cigar shape moving ahead.

"Turn onto one zero five," Wytton said. "The aircraft is now in your one-o'clock position five miles ahead."

I looked down over to the right of the aircraft's nose. Ambrose reluctantly looked out of the window in sulky silence.

"*There*," Kenny Bayst said. "Over there, down there." I looked where he was pointing . . . and there it was, slightly more over to our right, beginning another circling sweep over a darker patch of cloud which might have been a hole, but wasn't.

"Contact," I said to Wytton. "Closing in now."

"Your intentions?" he asked unemotionally.

"Lead them up to The Wash, descent over the sea,

follow the river and railway from King's Lynn to Cambridge."

"Roger. We'll advise Marham. They'll give you radar coverage over the sea."

I put the nose down, built up the speed, and overhauled the other aircraft like an E-type catching a bicycle. The nearer we got, the more I hoped. . . . It was a low-winged airplane . . . a Cherokee . . . white with red markings . . . and finally the registration number . . . and someone frantically waving a map at us from the window.

The relief was overpowering.

"It's them," Annie said, and I could only nod and swallow.

I throttled back and slowed the Six until it was down to Nancy's cruising speed, then circled until I came up on her left-hand side, and about fifty yards away. She had never done any formation flying. Fifty yards was the closest it was safe to go to her, and even fifty yards was risking it a bit. I kept my hand on the throttle, my eyes on her, and an extra pair of eyes I didn't know I had fixed on the heading.

To Annie Villars I said, "Hold up the letters for 'follow.' Slowly. One by one."

"Right." She held them flat against the window beside her. We could see Colin's head leaning back behind Nancy's. When Annie finished the word, we saw him wave his hand, and after that Nancy waved her map against her window, which showed up better.

"Wytton," I reported. "It is the right aircraft. They are following us to The Wash. Can you give me a steer to King's Lynn?"

"Delighted," he said. "Steer zero four zero, and call Marham on this frequency."

"Thanks a lot," I said with feeling.

"You're very welcome."

Good guys, I thought. Very good guys, sitting in their darkened rooms wearing headsets and staring at their little dark circular screens, watching the multitude of yellow-orange dots which were aircraft swimming slowly across like tadpoles. They'd done a terrific job finding the Rosses. Terrific.

"Can you make a figure 4?" I asked Annie Villars.

"Certainly." The scissors began to snip.

"When you have, would you hold up the 0, then the 4, then the 0 again?"

"With pleasure."

She held up the figures. Nancy waved the map. We set off northeastward to the sea, Nancy staying behind us to the right, with me flying looking over my shoulder to keep a steady distance between us. I judged it would take thirteen minutes at her speed to reach the sea, five to ten to let down, and twenty or so more to return underneath the cloud base to Cambridge. Her fuel by the time she got there would be low, but there was less risk of her running dry than of hitting a hill or trees or a building by going down over the land. Letting down over the sea was in these circumstances the best procedure whenever possible.

"We're going to need some more letters," I told Annie.

"Which?"

"Umm. . . . R, I, V, and N, D, C, and a T, and a 9."

"Right."

Out of the corner of my eye I could see Annie Villars snipping and Kenny Bayst, sitting behind her, sorting out the letters she had already made so that she could easily pick them out when they were needed. There was, I thought with a small internal smile, a truce in operation in that area.

Marham radar reported, "You have four miles to run to the coast."

"Hope the tide's in," I said facetiously.

"Affirmative," he said with deadpan humor. "High water eighteen forty hours. B.S.T."

"And . . . er . . . the cloud base?"

"Stand by." Down in his dark room, he couldn't see the sky. He had to ask the tower dwellers above.

"Cloud base between six and seven hundred feet

above sea level over the entire area from The Wash to Cambridge. Visibility two kilometers in drizzle."

"Nice," I said with irony.

"Very."

"Could I have the regional pressure settings?"

"Nine nine eight millibars."

"Nine nine eight," I repeated, and took my hand off the throttle long enough to set that figure on the subscale. To Annie Villars I said, "Can you make an 8, as well?"

"I expect so."

"Crossing the coast," Marham said.

"Right. . . . Miss Villars will you hold up S E A?"

She nodded and did so. Nancy waved the map.

"Now hold up S E T, then 9 9 8, then M B S."

"S . . . E . . . T," she repeated, holding them against the window. "Nine . . . nine . . . eight." She paused. "There's no M cut out."

"W upside down," Kenny Bayst said, and gave it to her.

"Oh, yes. M . . . B . . . S. What does MBS mean?"

"Millibars," I said.

Nancy waved the map, but I said to Annie, "Hold up the nine nine eight again, it's very important."

She held them up. We could see Nancy's head nodding as she waved back vigorously.

"Why is it so important?" Annie said.

"Unless you set the altimeter to the right pressure on the subscale, it doesn't tell you how high you are above the sea."

"Oh."

"Now would you hold up B A S E, then 6 0 0, then F T."

"Right. . . . Base . . . six hundred . . . feet."

There was a distinct pause before Nancy waved, and then it was a small, halfhearted one. She must have been horrified to find that the clouds were so low: she must have been thanking her stars that she hadn't tried to go down through them. Highly frightening piece of information, that six hundred feet.

141

"Now," I said to Annie, "hold up 'Follow river and rail one nine zero to Cambridge."

Follow . . . river . . . and . . . rail . . . one . . . nine . . . zero . . . to . . . Cambridge. . . . No G. . . . Never mind, C will do, then E." She spelt it out slowly. Nancy waved.

"And just one more . . . 4 0, then N, then M."

"Forty nautical miles," she said triumphantly. She held them up and Nancy waved.

"Now hold up 'follow' again."

"Right."

I consulted Marham, took Nancy out to sea a little further, and led her round in a circle until we were both heading just west of south on one nine zero, and in a straight line to the railway and river from King's Lynn to Cambridge.

"Hold up D O W N," I said.

She did it without speaking. Nancy gave a little wave. I put the nose of the six down toward the clouds and accelerated to a hundred and forty knots so that there would be no possibility of her crashing into the back of us. The white fleecy layer came up to meet us, embraced us in sunlit feathery wisps, closed lightly around us, became denser, darker, an anthracite fog pressing on the windows. The altimeter unwound, the clock needles going backward through 3,000 feet, 2,000 feet, 1,000 feet, still no break at 800 feet, 700 . . . and there, there at last the mist receded a little and became drizzly haze, and underneath us, pretty close underneath, were the restless rain-swept dark greeny-gray waves.

The passengers were all silent. I glanced round at them. They were all looking down at the sea in varying states of awe. I wondered if any of them knew I had just broken two laws and would undoubtedly be prosecuted again by the Board of Trade. I wondered if I would ever, ever learn to keep myself out of trouble.

We crossed the coast over King's Lynn and flew

down the river to Ely and Cambridge, just brushing through the misty cloud base at seven hundred feet. The forward visibility was bad, and I judged it silly to go back and wait for Nancy, because we might collide before we saw each other. I completed the journey as briefly as possible, and we landed on the wet tarmac and taxied round toward the airport buildings. When I stopped the engine, everyone, as if moved by one mind, climbed out and looked upward; even Ambrose.

The drizzle was light now, like fine mist. We stood quietly in it, getting damp, listening for the sound of an engine, watching for the shadow against the sky. Minutes ticked past. Annie Villars looked at me anxiously. I shook my head, not knowing exactly what I meant.

She couldn't have gone down too far . . . hit the sea . . . got disorientated in the cloud . . . lost when she came out of it . . . still in danger.

The drizzle fell. My heart also.

But she hadn't made any mistakes.

The engine noise crept in as a hum, then a buzz, then a definite rhythm. The little red-and-white airplane appeared suddenly against the right-hand sky, and she was circling safely round the outskirts of the field and coming sedately down to land.

"Oh. . . ." Annie Villars said, and wiped two surprising tears of relief out of her eyes.

Ambrose said sulkily, "That's all right, then. Now I hope we can get off home," and stomped heavily off toward the buildings.

Nancy taxied round and stopped her Cherokee a short distance away. Colin climbed out on the wing, grinned hugely in our direction, and waved.

"He's got no bloody nerves," Kenny said. "Not a bleeding nerve in his whole body."

Nancy came out after him, jumping down onto the tarmac and staggering a bit as she landed on her wobbly knees. I began to walk toward them. She started slowly to meet me, and then faster, and then ran, with her hair swinging out and her arms stretched wide. I grabbed her round the waist and swung her up and round in the air, and when I put her down she wrapped her arms behind my neck and kissed me.

"Matt. . . ." She was half laughing, half crying, her eyes shining, her cheeks a burning red, the sudden release of tension making her tremble down to her fingertips.

Colin reached us and gave me a pat on the shoulder.

"Thanks, chum."

"Thank the R.A.F. They found you on their radar."

"But how did you know? . . ."

"Long story," I said. Nancy was still holding on to me as if she would fall down if she let go. I made the most of it by kissing her again, on my own account.

She laughed shakily and untwined her arms. "When you came—I can't tell you—it was such a relief. . . ."

Annie Villars came up and touched her arm and she turned to her with the same hectic overexcitement.

"Oh . . . *Annie*."

"Yes, dear," she said calmly. "What you need now is a strong brandy."

"I ought to see to . . ." She looked vaguely in my direction, and back to her Cherokee.

"Colin and Matt will see to everything."

"All right, then. . . ." She let herself be taken off by Annie Villars, who had recovered her poise and assumed total command as a good general should. Kenny and the other jockey and trainer meekly followed.

"Now," said Colin. "How on earth did you know we needed you?"

"I'll show you," I said abruptly. "Come and look." I walked him back to the little Cherokee, climbed up onto the wing, and lay down on my back across the two front seats, looking up under the control panel.

"What on earth? . . ."

The device was there. I showed it to him. Very neat, very small. A little polyethylene-wrapped packet swinging free on a rubber band which was itself attached to the cable leading to the master switch. Nearer the switch, one wire of the two-wire cable had been bared: the two severed ends of copper showed readily against the black plastic casing.

I left everything where it was and eased myself out onto the wing.

"What is it? What does it mean?"

"Your electric system was sabotaged."

"For God's sake . . . Why?"

"I don't know." I sighed. "I only know who did it. The same person who planted the bomb a month ago. Major Rupert Tyderman."

He stared at me blankly. "It doesn't make sense."

"Not much. No."

I told him how the Major had set off the bomb while we were safely on the ground, and that today he had thought I was flying Nancy's Cherokee and could get myself out of trouble.

"But that's— That means—"

"Yes," I said.

"He's trying to make it look as though someone's trying to kill me."

I nodded. "While making damn sure you survive."

145

Chapter Eleven

The Board of Trade came down like the hounds of hell, and it wasn't the tall reasonable man I faced this time in the crew room but a short hard-packed individual with an obstinate jaw and unhumorous eyes. He refused to sit down: preferred to stand. He had brought no silent note taker along. He was strictly a one-man band. And hot on percussion.

"I must bring to your attention the Air Navigation Order 1966." His voice was staccato and uncompromising, the traditional politeness of his department reduced to the thinnest of veneers.

I indicated that I was reasonably familiar with the order in question. As it ruled every cranny of a professional pilot's life, this was hardly surprising.

"We have been informed that on Friday last you contravened Article Twenty-five, Paragraph Four, Subsection A, and Regulation Eight, Paragraph Two."

I waited for him to finish. Then I said, "Who informed you?"

He looked at me sharply. "That is beside the point."

"Could it have been Polyplanes?"

His eyelids flickered in spite of himself. "If we receive a complaint which can be substantiated, we are bound to investigate."

The complaint could be substantiated, all right. Saturday's newspapers were still strewn around the crew room this Monday morning, all full of the latest attempt on Colin Ross's life. Front-page stuff. Also minute details from all my passengers about how we had led him out to sea and brought him home under the 700-foot cloud base.

Only trouble was it was illegal in a single-engine airplane like the Six to take paying customers out over the sea as low as I had, and to land them at an airport where the cloud base was lower than one thousand feet.

"You admit that you contravened Article—"

I interrupted him. "Yes."

He opened his mouth and shut it again. "Er, I see." He cleared his throat. "You will receive a summons in due course."

"Yes," I said again.

"Not your first, I believe." An observation, not a sneer.

"No," I said unemotionally.

A short silence. Then I said, "How did that gadget work? The nitric-acid package on the rubber band."

"That is not your concern."

I shrugged. "I can ask any schoolboy who does chemistry."

He hesitated. He was not of the stuff to give anything away. He would never, as the tall man had, say or imply that there could be any fault in his Government or the Board. But, having searched his conscience and no doubt his standing orders, he felt able after all to come across.

"The package contained fluffy fiberglass soaked in a weak solution of nitric acid. A section of wire in the cable to the master switch had been bared, and the fiberglass wrapped around it. The nitric acid slowly dissolved the copper wire, taking, at that concentration, probably about an hour and a half to complete the process." He stopped, considering.

"And the rubber band?" I prompted.

"Yes. . . . Well, nitric acid, like water, conducts electricity, so that while the fiberglass was still in position the electrical circuit would be maintained, even though the wire itself had been completely dissolved. To break the circuit, the fiberglass package had to be removed. This was done by fastening it under tension via the rubber band to a point further up the cable. When the nitric acid dissolved right through the wire and the two ends parted, there was nothing to stop the rubber band contracting and pulling the fiberglass package away. Er . . . do I make myself clear?"

"Indeed," I agreed, "you do."

He seemed to give himself a little mental and physical shake, and turned with sudden energy toward the door.

"Right," he said briskly. "Then I need a word with Mr. Harley."

"Did you get a word with Major Tyderman?" I asked.

After the merest hiatus, he said again, "That is not your concern."

"Perhaps, you have seen him already?"

Silence.

"Perhaps, though, he is away from home?"

More silence. Then he turned to me in stiff exasperation. "It is not your business to question me like this. I cannot answer you any more. It is I who am here to inquire into you, not the other way round." He shut his mouth with a snap and gave me a hard stare. "And they even warned me," he muttered.

"I hope you find the Major," I said politely, "before he plants any more little devices in inconvenient places."

He snorted, and strode before me as we left the crew room and went along to Harley's office. Harley knew what he was there for and had been predictably furious with me ever since Friday.

"Mr. Shore admits the contraventions," the Board of Trade said.

"He'd be hard pushed not to," Harley said angrily, "considering every R.A.F. base across the country told him about the low cloud base at Cambridge."

"In point of fact," agreed the Board of Trade, "he should have returned immediately to Manchester, which was then still within the legal limit, and waited there until conditions improved, instead of flying all

the way to East Anglia and leaving himself with too
small a fuel margin to go on to any cloud-free airport.
The proper course was certainly to turn back right at
the beginning."

"And to hell with Colin Ross," I said conversationally.

Their mouth tightened in chorus. There was nothing more to be said. If you jumped red traffic lights
and broke the speed limit rushing someone to hospital to save his life, you could still be prosecuted for
the offenses. Same thing exactly. Same impasse. Hu-
manity versus law, an age-old quandary. Make your
choice and lie on it.

"I'm not accepting any responsibility for what you
did," Harley said heavily. "I will state categorically,
and in court if I have to, that you were acting in
direct opposition to Derrydowns' instructions, and
that Derrydowns disassociates itself entirely from
your actions."

I thought of asking him if he'd like a basin for the
ritual washing of hands. I also thought that on the
whole I'd better not.

He went on, "And of course if there is any fine
involved you will pay it yourself."

Always my bad luck, I reflected, to cop it when the
firm was too nearly bankrupt to be generous. I said
merely, "Is that all, then? We have a charter, if you
remember. . . ."

They waved me away in disgust, and I collected
my gear and flew off in the Aztec to take a clutch of
businessmen from Elstree to The Hague.

By the time, the previous Friday, that Colin and I
had locked Nancy's Cherokee and insured that no one
would touch it, the first cohorts of the local press had
come galloping up with ash on their shirt fronts, and
the Board of Trade, who neither slumbered nor slept,
were breathing heavily down the S.T.D.

Aircraft radios are about as private as Times
Square: it appeared that dozens of ground-based but

air-minded Midlands enthusiasts had been listening in to my conversation with Birmingham radar and had jammed the switchboard at Cambridge ringing up to find out if Colin Ross was safe. Undaunted, they had conveyed to Fleet Street the possibility of his loss. His arrival in one piece was announced on a television news broadcast forty minutes after we landed. The great British media had pulled out every finger they possessed. Nancy and Annie Villars had answered questions until their throats were sore, and had finally taken refuge in the Ladies' Cloaks. Colin was used to dealing with the press, but by the time he extricated himself from their ever-increasing news-hungry numbers he, too, was pale blue from tiredness.

"Come on," he said to me. "Let's get Nancy out and go home."

"I'll have to ring Harley...."

Harley already knew and was exploding like a fire-cracker. Someone from Polyplanes, it appeared, had telephoned at once to inform him with acid sweetness that his so highly qualified chief pilot had broken every law in sight and put Derrydowns thoroughly in the cart. The fact that his best customer was still alive to pay another day didn't seem to have got through to Harley at all. Polyplanes had made him smart, and it was all my fault.

I stayed in Cambridge by promising to foot the bill for hangarage again, and went home with Nancy and Colin.

Home.

A dangerous, evocative word. And the trouble was it *felt* like home. Only the third time I'd been there, and it was already familiar, cozy, undemanding, easy. ... It was no good feeling I belonged there, because I didn't.

Saturday morning I spent talking to the police face-to-face in Cambridge and the Board of Trade in London on the telephone. Both forces cautiously mur-

mured that they might perhaps ask Major Rupert
Tyderman to help them with their inquiries. Saturday
afternoon I flew Colin back to Haydock without incident; Saturday night I again stayed contentedly at
Newmarket; Sunday I took him to Buckingham,
changed over to the Aztec, and flew him to Ostend.
Managed to avoid Harley altogether until I got back
Sunday evening, when he lay in wait for me as I
taxied down to the hangar and bitched on for over
half an hour about sticking to the letter of the law.
The gist of his argument was that, left to herself,
Nancy would have come down safely somewhere
over the flat land of East Anglia. Bound to have
done. She wouldn't have hit any of the radio masts or
power-station chimneys which scattered the area and
which had stuck up into the clouds like needles. They
were all marked there, disturbing her, on the map.
She had known that if she had to go down at random
she had an average chance of hitting one. The television mast at Mendlesham stretched upward for more
than a thousand feet. ... But, said Harley, she would
have missed the lot. Certain to have done.

"What would you have felt like in her position?" I
asked.

He didn't answer. He knew well enough. As pilot, as
businessman, he was a bloody fool.

On Tuesday morning, he told me that Colin had
telephoned to cancel his trip to Folkestone that day,
but that I would still be going in the Six, taking an
owner and his friends there from Nottingham.

I imagined that Colin had changed his intention to
ride at Folkestone and gone to Pontefract instead, but
it wasn't so. He had, I found, flown to Folkestone. And
he had gone in a Polyplane.

I didn't know he was there until after the races,
when he came back to the airport in a taxi. He
climbed out of it in his usual wilted state, surveyed
the row of parked aircraft, and walked straight past
me toward the Polyplane.

"Colin," I said.

He stopped, turned his head, gave me a straight stare. Nothing friendly in it, nothing at all.

"What's the matter?" I said, puzzled. "What's happened?"

He looked away from me, along to the Polyplane. I followed his glance. The pilot was standing there smirking. He was the one who had refused to help Kenny Bayst, and he had been smirking vigorously all afternoon.

"Did you come with him?" I asked.

"Yes, I did." His voice was cold. His eyes also.

I said in surprise, "I don't get it. . . ."

Colin's face turned from cold to scorching. "You— you— I don't think I can bear to talk to you."

A feeling of unreality clogged my tongue. I simply looked at him in bewilderment.

"You've properly bust us up. . . . Oh, I dare say you didn't mean to . . . but Nancy has lit off out of the house and I left Midge at home crying. . . .

I was appalled. "But why? On Sunday morning when we left, everything was fine. . . ."

"Yesterday," he said flatly. "Nancy found out yesterday, when she went to the airfield for a practice session. It absolutely threw her. She came home in a dreadful mood and raged round the house, practically throwing things, and this morning she packed a suitcase and walked out. . . . Neither Midge nor I could stop her and Midge is frantically distressed—" He stopped, clenched his jaw, and said with shut teeth, "Why the hell didn't you have the guts to tell her yourself?"

"Tell her what?"

"*What?*" He thrust his hand into the pocket of his faded jeans and brought out a folded wad of newspaper. "This."

I took it from him. Unfolded it. Felt the woodenness take over in my face; knew that it showed.

He had handed me the most biting, the most damaging of the tabloid accounts of my trial and conviction for negligently putting the lives of eighty-seven

153

people in jeopardy. A one-day wonder to the general public; long forgotten. But always lying there in the files, if anyone wanted to dig it up.

"That wasn't all," Colin said. "He told her also that you'd been sacked from another airline for cowardice."

"Who told her?" I said dully. I held out the cutting. He took it back.

"Does it matter?"

"Yes, it does."

"He had no axe to grind. That's what convinced her."

"No axe to grind," I said bitterly. "That's a laugh."

"I believe so. What does it matter?"

"Was it a Polyplane pilot who told her? The one, for instance, who is flying you today?" Getting his own back, I thought, for the way I'd threatened him at Redcar.

Colin's mouth opened.

"No axe to grind," I said bitterly. "That's a laugh. They've been trying to pry you loose from Derrydowns all summer, and now it looks as if they've done it."

I turned away from him, my throat physically closing. I didn't think I could speak. I expected him to walk on, to walk away, to take himself to Polyplanes and my future to the trash can.

Instead of that, he followed me and touched my arm.

"Matt. . . ."

I shook him off. "You tell your precious sister," I said thickly, "that because of the rules I broke leading her back to Cambridge last Friday I am going to find myself in court again, and convicted and fined and in debt again . . . and this time I did it with my eyes open . . . not like that"—I pointed to the newspaper clipping with a hand that trembled visibly—"when I had to take the rap for something that was mostly not my fault."

"Matt!" He was himself appalled.

"And as for the cowardice bit, she's got her facts wrong. . . . Oh, I've no doubt it sounded convincing and dreadful—Polyplanes had a lot to gain by upsetting her to the utmost—but I don't see—I don't see why she was more upset than just to persuade you not to fly with me."

"Why didn't you tell her yourself?"

I shook my head. "I probably might have done, one day. I didn't think it was important."

"Not important!" He was fierce with irritation. "She seems to have been building up some sort of hero image of you, and then she discovered you had clay feet in all directions. . . . Of course you should have told her, as you were going to marry her. That was obviously what upset her most."

I was speechless. My jaw literally dropped. Finally I said foolishly, "Did you say *marry?*" . . .

"Well, yes, of course," he said impatiently, and then seemed struck by my state of shock. "You were going to marry her, weren't you?"

"We've never—even talked about it."

"But you must have," he insisted. "I overheard her and Midge discussing it on Sunday evening, after I got back from Ostend. 'When you are married to Matt,' Midge said. I heard her distinctly. They were in the kitchen, washing up. They were deciding you would come and live with us in the bungalow. . . . They were sharing out the bedrooms. . . ." His voice tailed off weakly. "It isn't—it isn't true?"

I silently shook my head.

He looked at me in bewilderment. "Girls," he said. "Girls."

"I can't marry her," I said numbly. "I've hardly enough for a license."

"That doesn't matter."

"It does to me."

"It wouldn't to Nancy," he said. He did a sort of double take. "Do you mean—she wasn't so far out—after all?"

"I suppose . . . not so far."

155

He looked down at the cutting in his hand, and suddenly screwed it up. "It looked so bad," he said with a tinge of apology.

"It was bad," I said.

He looked at my face. "Yes. I see it was."

A taxi drew up with a jerk and out piled my passengers, all gay and flushed with a winner and carrying a bottle of champagne.

"I'll explain to her," Colin said. "I'll get her back. ..." His expression was suddenly horrified. Shattered.

"Where has she gone?" I asked.

He screwed up his eyes as if in pain.

"She said"—he swallowed—"she went—to Chanter."

I sat all evening in the caravan wanting to smash something. Smash the galley. Smash the windows. Smash the walls.

Might have felt better if I had.

Chanter. ...

Couldn't eat, couldn't think, couldn't sleep.

Never had listened to my own advice: don't get involved. Should have stuck to it, stayed frozen. Icy. Safe.

Tried to get back to the arctic and not feel anything, but it was too late. Feeling had come back with a vengeance and of an intensity I could have done without.

I hadn't known I loved her. Knew I liked her, felt easy with her, wanted to be with her often and for a long time to come. I'd thought I could stop at friendship, and didn't realize how far, how deep I had already gone.

Oh, Nancy. ...

I went to sleep in the end by drinking half of the bottle of whisky Kenny Bayst had given me, but it didn't do much good. I woke up at six in the morning to the same dreary torment and with a headache on top.

156

There were no flights that day to take my mind off it.

Nancy and Chanter. . . .

At some point in the morning, I telephoned from the coin box in the customers' lounge to the art school in Liverpool, to ask for Chanter's home address. A crisp secretarial female voice answered: very sorry, absolutely not their policy to divulge the private addresses of their staff. If I could write, they would forward the letter.

"Could I speak to him, then, do you think?" I asked; though what good that would do, heaven alone knew.

"I'm afraid not, because he isn't here. The school is temporarily closed, and we are not sure when it will reopen."

"The students," I remembered, "are on strike?"

"That—er—is so," she agreed.

"Can't you possibly tell me how I could get in touch with Chanter?"

"Oh, dear. . . . You are the second person pressing me for help . . . but honestly, to tell you the truth, we don't know where he lives. . . . He moves frequently and seldom bothers to keep us up to date." Secretarial disapproval and despair in the tidy voice. "As I told Mr. Ross, with all the best will in the world, I simply have no idea where you could find him."

I sat in the crew room while the afternoon dragged by. Finished writing up all records by two-thirty, read through some newly arrived information circulars, calculated I had only three weeks and four days to run before my next medical, worked out that if I bought four cups of coffee every day from Honey's machine I was drinking away one-fifteenth of my total week's spending money, decided to make it water more often, looked up when Harley came stalking in, received a lecture on loyalty (mine to him), heard that I was on the next day to take a Wiltshire trainer to Newmarket races, and that if I gave Polyplanes any more grounds for reporting me or the firm to the Board of Trade, I could collect my cards.

"Do my best not to," I murmured. Didn't please him.

Looked at the door swinging shut behind his back.

Looked at the clock. Three-twenty-two.

Chanter and Nancy.

Back in the caravan, the same as the evening before. Tried turning on the television. Some comedy about American suburban life punctuated by canned laughter. Stood five minutes of it, and found the silence afterward almost as bad.

Walked halfway round the airfield, cut down to the village, drank half a pint in the pub, walked back. Total, four miles. When I stepped into the caravan, it was still only nine o'clock.

Honey Harley was waiting for me, draped over the sofa with maximum exposure of leg. Pink checked cotton sundress, very low cut.

"Hi," she said with self-possession. "Where've you been?"

"For a walk."

She looked at me quizically. "Got the Board of Trade on your mind?"

I nodded. That, and other things.

"I shouldn't worry too much. Whatever the law says or does, you couldn't have just left the Rosses to flounder."

"Your uncle doesn't agree."

"Uncle," she said dispassionately, "is a nit. And anyway play your cards right, and even if you do get a fine, Colin Ross will pay it. All you'd have to do would be to ask."

I shook my head.

"You're daft," she said. "Plain daft."

"You may be right."

She sighed, stirred, stood up. The curvy body rippled in all the right places. I thought of Nancy: much flatter, much thinner, less obviously sexed, and infinitely more desirable. I turned abruptly away from Honey. Like hitting a raw nerve, the thought of Chanter, with his hair and his fringes . . . and his hands.

"O.K., iceberg," she said mistakenly, "relax. Your virtue is quite safe. I only came down, to start with, to tell you there was a phone call for you, and would you please ring back."

"Who?" I tried hard to keep it casual.

"Colin Ross," Honey said matter-of-factly. "He wants you to call sometime this evening, if you can. I said if it was about a flight I could deal with it, but apparently it's something personal." She finished the sentence halfway between an accusation and a question and left me ample time to explain.

I didn't. I said, "I'll go up now, then, and use the telephone in the lounge."

She shrugged. "All right."

She walked up with me, but didn't quite have the nerve to hover close enough to listen. I shut the lounge door in front of her resigned and rueful face.

Got the number.

"Colin? Matt."

"Oh, good," he said. "Look. Nancy rang up today while Midge and I were at the races. . . . I took Midge along on the Heath because she was so miserable at home, and now of course she's even more miserable that she missed Nancy. . . . Anyway, our cleaning woman answered the telephone, and Nancy left a message."

"Is she—I mean, is she all right?"

"Do you mean, is she with Chanter?" His voice was strained. "She told our cleaner she had met an old art-school friend in Liverpool and was spending a few days camping with her near Warwick."

"*Her?*" I exclaimed.

"Well, I don't know. I asked our Mrs. Williams, and she then said she *thought* Nancy said 'her,' but of course she would think that, wouldn't she?"

"I'm afraid she would."

"But anyway Nancy had been much more insistent

that Mrs. Williams tell me something else. . . . It seems she has seen Major Tyderman."

"She didn't!"

"Yeah. . . . She said she saw Major Tyderman in the passenger seat of a car on the Stratford road out of Warwick. Apparently there were some roadworks, and the car stopped for a moment just near her."

"He could have been going anywhere . . . from anywhere."

"Yes," he agreed in depression. "I rang the police in Cambridge to tell them, but Nancy had already been through to them when she called home. All she could remember about the driver was that he wore glasses. She thought he might have had dark hair and perhaps a mustache. She only glanced at him for a second because she was concentrating on Tyderman. Also she hadn't taken the number, and she's hopeless on the make of cars, so altogether it wasn't a great deal of help."

"No. . . ."

"Anyway, she told Mrs. Williams she would be coming home on Saturday. She said if I would drive to Warwick races instead of flying, she would come home with me in the car."

"Well . . . thank God for that."

"If for nothing else," he said aridly.

Chapter Twelve

I flew the customers from Wiltshire to Newmarket and parked the Six as far as possible from the Polyplane. When the passengers had departed standward, I got out of the fuggy cabin and into the free air, lay propped on one elbow on the grass, loosened my tie, opened the neck of my shirt. Scorching-hot day, a sigh of wind over the Heath, a couple of small cumulus clouds defying evaporation, blue sky over the blue planet.

A suitable day for camping.

Wrenched my thoughts away from the profitless grind: Nancy despised me, despised herself, had chosen Chanter as a refuge, as a steadfast known quantity, had run away from the near-stranger who had not been what he seemed, and gone to where she knew she was wanted. Blind, instinctive, impulsive flight. Reckless, understandable, forgivable flight. . . .

I could take Chanter, I thought mordantly. I could probably take the thought and memory of Chanter, if only she would settle for me in the end.

It was odd that you had to lose something you didn't even know you had before you began to want it more than anything on earth.

Down at the other end of the row of aircraft, the Polyplane pilot was strolling about, smoking again. One of these fine days he would blow himself up. There was no smile in place that afternoon: even from a hundred yards one could detect the gloom in the heavy frowns he occasionally got rid of in my direction.

Colin had booked with Harley for the week ahead. Polyplanes must have been wondering what else they would have to do to get him back.

They played rough, no doubt of that. Informing on Derrydowns to the Board of Trade, discrediting their pilot, spreading smears that they weren't safe. But would they blow up a Derrydowns aircraft? Would they go as far as that?

They would surely have had to feel certain they would gain from it before they risked it. But in fact they hadn't gained. No one had demonstrably been frightened away from using Derrydowns, particularly not Colin Ross. If the bomb had been meant to look like an attack on Colin's life, why should Colin think he would be any safer in a Polyplane?

If they had blown up the aircraft with passengers aboard, *that* would have ruined Derrydowns. But even if they had been prepared to go that far, they wouldn't have chosen a flight with Colin Ross on it.

And why Major Tyderman, when their own pilots could get near the Derrydowns aircraft without much comment? That was easier . . . they needed a bomb expert. Someone completely unsuspectible. Someone even their pilots didn't know. Because if the boss of Polyplanes had taken the dark step into crime, he wouldn't want chatty employees like pilots spilling it into every aviation bar from Prestwick to Lydd.

The second airplane, though, that Tyderman had sabotaged, hadn't been one of Derrydowns' at all. On the other hand, he had thought it was. I stood up, stretched, watched the straining horses scud through the first race, saw in the distance a girl with dark hair and a blue dress, and thought for one surging moment it was Nancy. It wasn't Nancy. It wasn't even Midge. Nancy was in Warwickshire, living in a tent.

I thrust my balled fists into my pockets. Not the slightest use thinking about it. Concentrate on something else. Start from the bottom again, as before. Look at everything the wrong way up.

No easy revelation this time. Just the merest flicker of speculation.

Harley? . . .

He had recovered ill-invested capital on the first occasion. He had known Colin would not rely often on his sister's skill after the second. But would Harley go so far? . . . And Harley had known I wasn't flying Colin, though Tyderman had thought I was.

Rats on treadwheels, I thought, go round and round in small circles and get nowhere, just like me.

I sighed. It wasn't much use trying to work it all out when I obviously lacked about fifty pieces of vital information. Decision: did I or did I not start actively looking for some of the pieces? If I didn't a successor to Major Tyderman might soon be around playing another lot of chemical tricks on airplanes, and if I did, I could well be heading myself for yet more trouble.

I tossed an imaginary coin. Heads you do, tails you don't. In mid-toss I thought of Nancy. All roads led back to Nancy. If I just let everything slide and lay both physically and metaphorically on my back on the grass in the sun, I'd have nothing to think about except what I hated to think about. Very poor prospect. Almost everything else was better.

Took the plunge, and made a start with Annie Villars.

She was standing in the paddock in a sleeveless dark red dress, her graying short hair curling neatly under a black straw hat chosen more for generalship than feminity. From ten paces, the authority was clearly uppermost: from three, one could hear the incongruously gentle voice, see the nonaggression in the consciously curved lips, realize that the velvet glove was being given a quilted lining.

She was talking to the Duke of Wessex. She was saying, "Then if you agree, Bobbie, we'll ask Kenny Bayst to ride it. This new boy had no judgment of

163

pace, and, for all his faults, Kenny does know how to
time a race."

The Duke nodded his distinguished head and
smiled at her benevolently. They caught sight of me
hovering near them and both turned toward me with
friendly expressions, one deceptively and one authen-
tically vacant.

"Matt," said the Duke, smiling. "My dear chap.
Isn't it a splendid day?"

"Beautiful, sir," I agreed. As long as one could
obliterate Warwickshire.

"My nephew Matthew," he said. "Do you remember him?"

"Of course I do, sir."

"Well—it's his birthday soon, and he wants—he was
wondering if for a birthday present I would give him
a flight in an airplane. With you, he said. Especially
with you."

I smiled. "I'd like to do that very much."

"Good, good. Then—er—how do you suggest we fix
it?"

"I'll arrange it with Mr. Harley."

"Yes. Good. Soon, then. He's coming down to stay
with me tomorrow, as it's the end of term and his
mother is off somewhere in Greece. So next week,
perhaps?"

"I'm sure that will be all right."

He beamed happily. "Perhaps I'll come along, too."

Annie Villars said patiently, "Bobbie, we ought to
go and see about saddling your horse."

He looked at his watch. "By Jove, yes. Amazing
where the afternoon goes to. Come along, then." He
gave me another large smile, transferred it intact to
Annie, and obediently moved off after her as she
started purposefully toward the saddling boxes.

I bought a race card. The Duke's horse was a
two-year-old maiden called Thundersticks. I watched
the Duke and Annie watch Thundersticks walk round
the paddock, one with innocent beaming pride, the
other with judicious noncommitment. The pacelack-
ing boy rode a bad race, even to my unpracticed eye;

too far out in front over the first furlong, too far out
the back over the last. Just as well the Duke's colors
were inconspicuous, I thought. He took his disappoint-
ment with charming grace, reassuring Annie that the
colt would do better next time. Sure to. Early days
yet. She smiled back at him in soft agreement, and
bestowed on the jockey a look which would have
bored a hole through steel plating.

After they had discussed the sweating colt's per-
formance yard by yard, and patted him and packed
him off with his lad toward the stables, the Duke took
Annie away to the bar for a drink. After that, she had
another loser for another owner, and another thoughtful detour for refreshment, so that I didn't manage to
catch her on her own until between the last two
races.

She listened without comment to me explaining
that I thought it might be possible to do something
positive about solving the Great Bomb Mystery, if she
would help.

"I thought it was solved already."

"Not really. No one knows why."

"No. Well, I don't see how I can help."

"Would you mind telling me how well Major Tyderman and Mr. Goldenberg know each other, and
how they come to have any say in how Rudiments
should run in its various races?"

She said mildly, "It's none of your business."

I knew what the mildness concealed. "I know
that."

"And you are impertinent."

"Yes."

She regarded me straightly, and the softness gradually faded out of her features to leave taut skin over
the cheekbones and a stern set to the mouth.

"I am fond of Midge and Nancy Ross," she said. "I
don't see how anything I can tell you will help, but I
certainly want no harm to come to those two girls.
That last escapade was just a shade too dangerous,
wasn't it? And if Rupert Tyderman could do that . . ."

165

She paused, thinking deeply. "I will be obliged if you will keep anything I may tell you to yourself."

"I will."

"Very well. . . . I've known Rupert for a very long time. More or less from my childhood. He is about fifteen years older. . . . When I was a young girl, I thought he was a splendid person, and I didn't understand why people hesitated when they talked about him." She sighed. "I found out, of course, when I was older. He had been wild, as a youth. A vandal when vandalism wasn't as common as it is now. When he was in his twenties, he borrowed money from all his relations and friends for various grand schemes, and never paid them back. His family bought him out of one mess where he had sold a picture entrusted to him for safekeeping and spent the proceeds. . . . Oh, lots of things like that. Then the war came and he volunteered immediately, and I believe all during the war he did very well. He was in the Royal Engineers, I think . . . but afterward, after the war ended, he was quietly allowed to resign his commission for cashing dud checks with his fellow officers."

She shook her head impatiently. "He has always been a fool to himself. . . . Since the war, he has lived on some money his grandfather left in trust, and on what he could cadge from any friends he had left."

"You included?" I suggested.

She nodded. "Oh, yes. He's always very persuasive. It's always for something extremely plausible, but all the deals fall through. . . ." She looked away across the Heath, considering. "And then this year, back in February or March, I think, he turned up one day and said he wouldn't need to borrow any more from me, he'd got a good thing going which would make him rich."

"What was it?"

"He wouldn't say. Just told me not to worry, it was all legal. He had gone into partnership with someone with a cast-iron idea for making a fortune. Well, I'd heard that sort of thing from him so often before. The only difference was that this time he didn't want money. . . ."

"He wanted something else?"

"Yes." She frowned. "He wanted me to introduce him to Bobbie Wessex. He said—just casually—how much he'd like to meet him, and I suppose I was so relieved not to find him cadging five hundred or so that I instantly agreed. It was very silly of me, but it didn't seem important. . . ."

"What happened then?"

She shrugged. "They were both at the Doncaster meeting at the opening of the flat season, so I introduced them. Nothing to it. Just a casual racecourse introduction. And then"—she looked annoyed—"the next time Rupert turned up with that man Goldenberg, saying Bobbie Wessex had given him permission to decide how Rudiments should be run in all his races. I said he certainly wasn't going to do that, and telephoned to Bobbie. But," she said, sighing, "Rupert had indeed talked him into giving him carte blanche with Rudiments. Rupert is an expert persuader, and Bobbie—well, poor Bobbie is easily open to suggestion. Anyone with half an eye could see that Goldenberg was as straight as a corkscrew, but Rupert said he was essential, as someone had got to put the bets on and he, Rupert, couldn't, as no bookmaker would accept his credit and you had to have hard cash for the Tote."

"And then the scheme went wrong," I said.

"The first time Rudiments won, they'd both collected a lot of money. I had told them the horse would win. Must win. It started at a hundred to six, first time out, and they were both as high as kites afterward."

"And next time Kenny Bayst won again, when he wasn't supposed to, when they had laid it?"

She looked startled. "So you did understand what they were saying."

"Eventually."

"Just like Rupert to let it out. No sense of discretion."

I sighed. "Well, thank you very much for being so frank. Even if I still can't see what connection Rudiments has with Major Tyderman blowing up one aircraft and crippling another."

She twisted her mouth. "I told you," she said, "right at the beginning that nothing I told you would be of any help."

Colin stopped beside me in pink-and-green silks on his way from the weighing room to the paddock for the last race. He gave me a concentrated inquiring look which softened into something like compassion.

"The waiting's doing you no good," he said.

"Has she telephoned again?"

He shook his head. "Midge won't leave the house, in case she does."

"I'll be at Warwick races on Saturday—flying some people up from Kent. . . . Will you ask her—just to talk to me?"

"I'll wring her stupid little neck," he said.

I flew the customers back to Wiltshire and the Six back to Buckingham. Harley, waiting around with bitter eyes, told me the Board of Trade had let him know they were definitely proceeding against me.

"I expected they would."

"But that's not what I wanted to speak to you about. Come into the office." He was unfriendly, as usual. Snappy. He picked up a sheet of paper from his desk and waved it at me.

"Look at these times. I've been going through the bills Honey has sent out since you've been here. All the times are shorter. We've had to charge less. . . . We're not making enough profit. It's got to stop. D'you understand? Got to stop."

"Very well."

He looked nonplused: hadn't expected such an easy victory.

"And I'm taking on another pilot."

"Am I out, then?" I found I scarcely cared.

He was surprised. "No. Of course not. We simply seem to be getting too much taxi work just lately for you to handle on your own, even with Don's help."

"Maybe we're getting more work because we're doing the trips faster and charging less," I suggested.

He was affronted. "Don't be ridiculous."

Another long evening in the caravan, aching and empty.

Nowhere to go, no way of going, and nothing to spend when I got there. That didn't matter, because wherever I went, whatever I spend, the inescapable thoughts lay in wait. Might as well suffer them alone and cheaply as anywhere else.

For something to do, I cleaned the caravan from end to end. When it was finished, it looked better, but I, on the whole, felt worse. Scrambled myself two eggs, ate them unenthusiastically on toast. Drank a dingy cup of dried coffee, dried milk.

Switched on the television. Old movie, *circa* 1950, pirates, cutlasses, heaving bosoms. Switched off.

Sat and watched night arrive on the airfield. Tried to concentrate on what Annie Villars had told me, so as not to think of night arriving over the fields and tents of Warwickshire. For a long time, had no success at all.

Look at everything upside down. Take absolutely nothing for granted.

The middle of the night produced out of a shallow restless sleep a singularly wild idea. Most sleep-spawned revelations from the subconscious wither and die to ridicule in the dawn, but this time it was different. At five, six, seven o'clock, it still looked possible. I traipsed in my mind through everything I had seen and heard since the day of the bomb, and added a satisfactory answer to *why* and the answer to *who* and *when*.

That Friday, I had to set off early in the Aztec to Germany with some television cameramen from Denham, wait while they took their shots, and bring them home again. In spite of breaking Harley's ruling about speed into pin-sized fragments, it was seven-thirty before I climbed stiffly out of the cockpit and helped Joe push the sturdy twin into the hangar.

"Need it for Sunday, don't you?" he asked.

"That's right. Colin Ross to France." I stretched and yawned, and picked up my heavy flight bag with all its charts and documents.

"We're working you hard."

"What I'm here for."

He put his hands in his overall pockets. "You're light on those airplanes, I'll give you that. Larry, now— Larry was heavy-handed. Always needing things repaired, we were, before you came."

I gave him a sketch of an appreciative smile and walked up to fill in the records in the office. Harley and Don were both still flying. Harley giving a lesson, and Don a sightseeing trip in the Six, and Honey was still traffic-copping in the tower. I climbed up there to see her and ask her a considerable favor.

"Borrow my Mini?" she repeated in surprise. "Do you mean now, this minute?"

I nodded. "For the evening."

"I suppose I could get Uncle to take me home," she reflected. "If you'll fetch me in the morning?"

"Certainly."

"Well . . . all right. I don't really need it this evening. Just fill it up with petrol before you hand it back."

"O.K. And thanks a lot."

She gave me a frankly vulgar grin. "Minis are too small for what you want."

I managed to grin back. "Yeah. . . ."

Given the wheels, make the appointment. A pleasant male voice answered the telephone, polite and quiet.

"The Duke of Wessex? Yes, this is his house. Who is speaking, please?"

"Matthew Shore."

"One moment, sir."

The one moment stretched to four minutes, and I fed a week's beer money into the greedy box. At last the receiver at the other end was picked up and, with slightly heavy breathing, the Duke's unmistakable voice said, "Matt? My dear chap, what can I do for you?"

"If you are not busy this evening, sir, could I call in to see you for a few minutes?"

"This evening? Busy? Hmm. . . . Is it about young Matthew's flight?"

"No, sir, something different. I won't take up much of your time."

"Come by all means, my dear chap, if you want to. After dinner, perhaps? Nine o'clock, say?"

"Nine o'clock," I confirmed. "I'll be there."

The Duke lived near Royston, west of Cambridge. Honey's Mini ate up the miles like Billy Bunter, so that it was nine o'clock exactly when I stopped at a local garage to ask for directions to the Duke's house. On Honey's radio someone was reading the news. I listened idly at first while the attendant finished filling up the car in front, and then with sharp and sickened attention. "Race-horse trainer Jarvis Kitch and owner Dobson Ambrose, whose filly Scotchbright won the Oaks last month, were killed today in a multiple traffic accident just outside Newmarket. The Australian jockey Kenny Bayst, who was in the car with them, was taken to hospital with multiple injuries. His condition tonight is said to be fair. Three stable lads, trapped when a lorry crushed their car, also died in the crash."

Mechanically I asked for, got, and followed, the directions to the Duke's house. I was thinking about poor large aggressive Ambrose and his cowed trainer Kitch, hoping that Kenny wasn't too badly hurt to race again, and trying to foresee the ramifications.

171

There was nothing else on the news except for the weather forecast: heat wave indefinitely continuing.

No mention of Rupert Tyderman. But Tyderman, that day, *had* been seen by the police.

Chapter Thirteen

The Duke's manservant was as pleasant as his voice: a short, assured, slightly popeyed man in his late forties with a good deal of the Duke's natural benevolence in his manner. The house he presided over opened to the public, a notice read, every day between 1st March and 30th November. The Duke, I discovered, lived privately in the upper third of the southwest wing.

"The Duke is expecting you, sir. Will you come this way?"

I followed. The distance I followed accounted for the length of time I had waited for the Duke to come to the telephone and also his breathlessness when he got there. We went up three floors, along a two-furlong straight, and up again, to the attics. The attics in eighteenth-century stately homes were a long way from the front hall.

The manservant opened a white-painted door and gravely showed me in.

"Mr. Shore, Your Grace."

"Come in, come in, my dear chap," said the Duke.

I went in, and smiled with instant, spontaneous delight. The square low-ceilinged room contained a vast toy electric-train set laid out on an irregular ring of wide green-covered trestle tables. A terminus, sidings, two small towns, a branch line, tunnels, gradients, viaducts—the Duke had the lot. In the center of the ring, he and his nephew Matthew stood behind a large control table pressing the switches which sent about six different trains clanking on different courses round the complex.

The Duke nudged his nephew. "There you are, what did we say? He likes it."

Young Matthew gave me a fleeting glance and went back to some complicated points-changing. "He was bound to. He's got the right sort of face."

The Duke said, "You can crawl in here best under that table with the signal box and level crossing." He pointed, so I went down on hands and knees and made the indicated journey. Stood up in the center. Looked around at the rows of lines and remembered the hopeless passion I'd felt in toyshops as a child: my father had been an underpaid schoolmaster who had spent his money on books.

The two enthusiasts showed me where the lines crossed and how the trains could be switched without crashing. Their voices were filled with contentment, their eyes shining, their faces intent.

"Built this lot up gradually, of course," the Duke said. "Started when I was a boy. Then for years I never came up here. Not until young Matthew got old enough. Now, as I expect you can see, we have great times."

"We're thinking of running a branch line right through that wall over there into the next attic," Matthew said. "There isn't much more room in here."

The Duke nodded. "Next week, perhaps. For your birthday."

Young Matthew gave him a huge grin and deftly let a Pullman cross three seconds in front of a chugging goods. "It's getting dark," he observed. "Lighting-up time."

"So it is," agreed the Duke.

Matthew with a flourish pressed a switch, and they both watched my face. All round the track, and on all the stations and signal boxes and in the signals themselves, tiny electric lights suddenly shone out. The effect, to my eyes, was enchanting.

"There you are," said the Duke. "He likes it."

174

"Bound to," young Matthew said.

They played with the trains for another whole hour, because they had worked out a timetable and they wanted to see if they could keep to it before they pinned it up on the notice board in the terminal. The Duke apologized, not very apologetically, for keeping me waiting, but it was, he explained, Matthew's first evening out of school, and they had been waiting all through the term for this occasion.

At twenty to eleven, the last shuttle service stopped at the buffers in the terminal and Matthew yawned. With the satisfaction of a job well done, the two railwaymen unfolded several large dust sheets and laid them carefully over the silent tracks, and then we all three crawled back under the table which held the level crossing.

The Duke led the way down the first flight and along the two furlongs, and we were then, it appeared, in his living quarters.

"You'd better cut along to bed now, Matthew," he said to his nephew. "See you in the morning. Eight o'clock sharp, out in the stables."

"Sure thing," Matthew said. "And after that the races." He sighed with utter content. "Better than school," he said.

The Duke showed me into a smallish white-painted sitting room furnished with Persian rugs, leather armchairs, and endless sporting prints.

"A drink?" he suggested, indicating a tray.

I looked at the bottles. "Whisky, please."

He nodded, poured two, added water, gave me the glass, and waved me to an armchair.

"Now, my dear chap? . . ."

It suddenly seemed difficult, what I had come to ask him, and what to explain. He was so transparently honest, so incapable of double-dealing: I wondered if he could comprehend villainy at all.

"I was talking to Annie Villars about your horse Rudiments," I said.

A slight frown lowered his eyebrows. "She was annoyed with me for letting her friend Rupert Tyder-

175

man advise me. . . . I do so dislike upsetting Annie, but I'd promised. . . . Anyway, she has sorted it all out splendidly, I believe, and now that her friend has turned out to be so extraordinary—with that bomb, I mean—I don't expect he will want to advise me about Rudiments any more."

"Did he, sir, introduce to you any friend of his?"

"Do you mean Eric Goldenberg? Yes, he did. Can't say I really liked the fellow, though. Didn't trust him, you know. Young Matthew didn't like him, either."

"Did Goldenberg ever talk to you about insurance?"

"Insurance?" he repeated. "No, I can't remember especially that he did."

I frowned. It had to be insurance.

It had to be.

"It was his other friend," said the Duke, "who arranged the insurance."

I stared at him. "Which other friend?"

"Charles Carthy-Todd."

I blinked. "Who?"

"Charles Carthy-Todd," he repeated patiently. "He was an acquaintance of Rupert Tyderman's. Tyderman introduced us one day. At Newmarket races, I think it was. Anyway, it was Charles who suggested the insurance. Very good scheme, I thought it was. Sound. Very much needed. An absolute boon to a great many people."

"The Racegoers' Accident Fund," I said. "Of which you are patron."

"That's right." He smiled. "So many people have complimented me on giving it my name. A splendid undertaking altogether."

"Could you tell me a little more about how it was set up?"

"Are you interested in insurance, my dear chap? I could get you an introduction at Lloyd's . . . but . . ."

I smiled. To become an underwriter at Lloyd's, one had to think of a stake of a hundred thousand pounds as loose change. The Duke, in his quiet good-natured way, was a very rich man indeed.

"No, sir. It's just the Accident Fund I'm interested in. How it was set up, and how it is run."

"Charles sees to it all, my dear chap. I can't seem to get the hang of these things at all, you know. Technicalities, and all that. Much prefer horses, don't you see?"

"Yes, sir, I do see. Could you perhaps, then, tell me about Mr. Carthy-Todd? What he's like, and so on."

"He's about your height but much heavier and he has dark hair and wears spectacles. I think he has a mustache. . . . Yes, that's right, a mustache."

I was jolted. The Duke's description of Charles Carthy-Todd fitted almost exactly the impression Nancy had had of Tyderman's companion. Dozens of men around, though, with dark hair, mustaches, glasses. . . .

"I really meant, sir, his—er—character."

"My dear chap. Sound. Very sound. A thoroughly good fellow. An expert in insurance, spent years with a big firm in the City."

"And—his background?" I suggested.

"Went to Rugby. Then straight into an office. Good family, of course."

"You've met them?"

He looked surprised at the question. "Not actually, no. Business connection, that's what I have with Charles. His family came from Herefordshire, I think. There are photographs in our office. . . . Land, horses, dogs, wife and children—that sort of thing. Why do you ask?"

I hesitated. "Did he come to you with the accident scheme complete?"

He shook his fine head. "No, no, my dear chap. It arose out of conversation. We were saying how sad it was for the family of that small steeplechase trainer who was drowned on holiday and what a pity it was that there wasn't some scheme which covered everyone engaged in racing, not just the jockeys. Then of course when we really went into it, we broadened it to include the racing public as well. Charles explained that the more premiums we collected the more we could pay out in compensation."

"I see."

"We have done a great deal of good already." He smiled happily. "Charles was telling me the other day that we have settled three claims for injuries so far, and that those clients are so pleased that they are telling everyone else to join in."

I nodded. "I've met one of them. He'd broken his ankle and received a thousand pounds."

He beamed. "There you are, then."

"When did the scheme actually start?"

"Let me see. In May, I should think. Toward the end of May. About two months ago. It took a little while to organize, of course, after we'd decided to go ahead."

"Charles did the organizing?"

"My dear chap, of course."

"Did you take advice from any of your friends at Lloyd's?"

"No need, you know. Charles is an expert himself. He drew up all the papers. I just signed them."

"But you read them first?"

"Oh, yes," he said reassuringly, then smiled like a child. "Didn't understand them much, of course."

"And you yourself guaranteed the money?" Since the collapse of cut-price car-insurance firms, I'd read somewhere, privately run insurance schemes had to show a minimum backing of fifty thousand pounds before the Board of Trade would give them permission to exist.

"That's right."

"Fifty thousand pounds?"

"We thought a hundred thousand might be better. Gives the scheme better standing, more weight, don't you see?"

"Charles said so?"

"He knows about such things."

"Yes."

"But of course I'll never have to find that money. It's only a guarantee of good faith, and to comply with the law. The premiums will cover the compensation and Charles's salary and all the costs. Charles worked it all out. And I told him right at the beginning that I didn't want any profit out of it just for lending it my name. I really don't need any profit. I told him just to add my share into the paying-out fund, and he thought that was a most sensible suggestion. Our whole purpose, you see, is to do good."

"You're a singularly kind, thoughtful, and generous man, sir," I said.

It made him uncomfortable. "My dear chap . . ."

"And after tonight's news, I think several widows in Newmarket will bless you."

"What news?"

I told him about the accident in which Kitch and Ambrose and the three stable lads had died. He was horrified.

"Oh, the poor fellows. The poor fellows. One can only hope that you are right, and that they had joined our scheme."

"Will the premiums you have already collected be enough to cover many large claims all at once?"

He wasn't troubled. "I expect so. Charles will have seen to all that. But even if they don't, I will make up the difference. No one will suffer. That's what guaranteeing means, do you see?"

"Yes, sir."

"Kitch and Ambrose," he said. "The poor fellows."

"And Kenny Bayst is in hospital, badly hurt."

"Oh dear." His distress was genuine. He really cared.

"I know that Kenny Bayst was insured with you. At least, he told me he was going to be. And after this I should think you would be flooded with more applications."

"I expect you're right. You seem to understand things, just like Charles does."

"Did Charles have any plans for giving the scheme a quick boost to begin with?"

"I don't follow you, my dear chap."

"What happened to the Accident Fund," I asked

casually, "after that bomb exploded in the airplane which had been carrying Colin Ross?"

He looked enthusiastic. "Do you know, a lot of people told me they would join. It made them think, they said. I asked Charles if they had really done anything about it, and he said yes, quite a few inquiries had come in. I said that as no one had been hurt, the bomb seemed to have done the Fund a lot of good, and Charles was surprised and said so it had."

Charles had met the Duke through Rupert Tyderman. Rupert Tyderman had set off the bomb. If ever there was a stone-cold certainty, it was that Charles Carthy-Todd was the least surprised on earth that cash had followed combustion. He had reckoned it would. He had reckoned right.

"Charles sent out a pamphlet urging everyone to insure against bombs on the way home," I said.

The Duke smiled. "Yes, that's right. I believe it was very effective. We thought, do you see, that as no one had been hurt, there would be no harm in it."

"And as it was Colin Ross who was on board, the bomb incident was extensively covered on television and in the newspapers . . . and had a greater impact on your Fund than had it been anyone else."

The Duke's forehead wrinkled. "I'm not sure I understand."

"Never mind, sir. I was just thinking aloud."

"Very easy habit to fall into. Do it myself, you know, all the time."

Carthy-Todd and Tyderman's second sabotage, I thought, hadn't been as good. Certainly by attacking Colin they'd achieved the same impact and national coverage, but I would have thought it was too obviously slanted at one person to have had much universal effect. Could be wrong, though. . . .

"This has been the most interesting chat," said the Duke. "But, my dear fellow, the evening is passing. What was it that you wanted to see me about?"

"Er . . ." I cleared my throat. "Do you know, sir, I'd very much like to meet Mr. Carthy-Todd. He sounds a most go-ahead, enterprising man."

The Duke nodded warmly.

"Do you know where I could find him?"

"Tonight, do you mean?" He was puzzled.

"No, sir. Tomorrow will do."

"I suppose you might find him at our office. He's sure to be there, because he knows I will be calling in myself. Warwick races, do you see?"

"The Accident Fund office . . . is in Warwick?"

"Of course."

"Silly of me," I said. "I didn't know."

The Duke twinkled at me. "I see you haven't joined the Fund."

"I'll join tomorrow. I'll go to the office. I'll be at Warwick, too, for the races."

"Great," he said. "Great. The office is only a few hundred yards from the racecourse." He put two fingers into an inside pocket and brought out a visiting card. "There you are, my dear chap. The address. And if you're there about an hour before the first race, I'll be there, too, and you can meet Charles. You'll like him. I'm sure of that."

"I'll look forward to it," I said. I finished my whisky and stood up. "It was kind of you to let me come . . . and I think your trains are absolutely splendid. . . ."

His face brightened. He escorted me all the way down to the front door, talking about young Matthew and the plans they had for the holidays. Would I fix Matthew's flight for Thursday, he asked. Thursday was Matthew's birthday. He would be eleven.

"Thursday it is," I agreed. "I'll do it in the evening if there's a charter fixed for that day."

"Most good of you, my dear chap."

I looked at the kind, distinguished, uncomprehending face. I knew that if his partner Charles Carthy-Todd skipped with the accumulated premiums before paying out the Newmarket widows, as I was privately certain he would, the Honourable Duke of Wessex would meet every penny out of his own coffers. In all probability he could afford it, but that wasn't the point. He would be hurt and bewildered and impossibly distressed at having been tangled up in a fraud, and it seemed to me especially vicious that anyone should take advantage of his vulnerable simplicity and goodness.

Charles Carthy-Todd was engaged in taking candy from a child and then making it look as though the child had stolen it in the first place. One couldn't help but feel protective. One couldn't help but want to stop it.

I said impulsively, "Take care of yourself, sir."

"My dear chap . . . I will."

I walked down the steps from his front door toward Honey's Mini waiting in the drive, and looked back to where he stood in the yellow oblong of light. He waved a hand gently, and slowly closed the door, and I saw from his benign but slightly puzzled expression that he was still not quite sure why I had come.

It was after one o'clock when I got back to the caravan. Tired, hungry, miserable about Nancy, I still couldn't stay asleep. Four o'clock I was awake again, tangling the sheets as if in fever. I got up and splashed my itching eyes with cold water: lay down, got up, went for a walk across the airfield. The cool starry night came through my shirt and soothed my skin but didn't do much for the hopeless ache between my ears.

At eight in the morning, I went to fetch Honey after filling her tank with the promised petrol at the nearest garage. She had made a gallon or two on the deal, I calculated. Fair enough.

What was not fair enough, however, was the news with which she greeted me.

"Colin Ross wants you to ring him up. He rang yesterday evening about half an hour after you'd buzzed off."

"Did he say . . . what about?"

"He did ask me to give you a message, but honestly I forgot. I was up in the tower until nine, and then Uncle was impatient to get home, and I just went off with him and forgot about coming down here with the message . . . and anyway what difference would a few hours make?"

"What was the message?"

"He said to tell you his sister didn't meet anyone called Chanter at Liverpool. Something about a strike, and this Chanter not being there. I don't know . . . there were two aircraft in the circuit and I wasn't paying all that much attention. Come to think if it, he did seem pretty anxious I should give you the message last night, but, like I said, I forgot. Sorry, and all that. Was it important?"

I took a deep breath. Thinking about the past night, I could cheerfully have strangled her. "Thanks for telling me."

She gave me a sharp glance. "You look bushed. Have you been making love all night? You don't look fit to fly."

"Seldom felt better," I said with truth. "And no, I haven't."

"Save yourself for me."

"Don't bank on it."

"Beast."

When I rang Colin's number from the telephone in the lounge, it was Midge who answered. The relief in her voice was as overwhelming as my own.

"Matt! . . ." I could hear her gulp, and knew she was fighting against tears. "Oh, Matt—I'm so glad you've rung. She didn't go after Chanter. She didn't. It's all right. Oh dear . . . just a minute. . . ." She sniffed and paused, and when she spoke again she had her voice under control. "She rang yesterday evening and we talked to her for a long time. She said she was sorry if she had upset us, she had really left because she was so angry with herself, so humiliated at having made up such silly dreams about you. . . . She said it was all her own fault, that you hadn't deceived her in any way, she had deceived herself. . . She wanted to tell us that it wasn't because she was angry with you that she ran out, but because she felt she had made such a fool of herself. . . . Anyway, she said she had cooled off a good deal by the time her train got to Liverpool and she was simply miserable by then, and then when she found Chanter had gone away because of the strike, she said she was relieved, really. Chanter's landlady told Nancy where he had gone—somewhere in Manchester, to do a painting of industrial chimneys, she thought—but Nancy decided it wasn't Chanter she wanted. . . . And she didn't know what to do, she still felt muddled. . . . And then outside the art school she met a girl who had been a student with us in London. She was setting off for a camping holiday near Stratford and—well—Nancy decided to go with her. She said a few days' peace and some landscape painting would put her right . . . so she rang up here, and it was our cleaning woman who answered. . . . Nancy swears she told her it was Jill she was with, and not Chanter, but of course we never got that part of the message . . ." She stopped, and when I didn't answer immediately she said anxiously, "Matt, are you still there?"

"Yes."

"You were so quiet."

"I was thinking about the last four days."

Four wretched, dragging days. Four endless, grinding nights. All unnecessary. She hadn't been with Chanter at all. If she'd suffered about what she'd imagined about me, so had I from what I'd imagined about her. Which made us, I guessed, about quits.

"Colin told her she should have asked you about that court case instead of jumping to conclusions," Midge said.

"She didn't jump, she was pushed."

"Yes. She knows that now. She's pretty upset. She doesn't really want to have to face you at Warwick—after making such a mess of things. . . ."

"I shan't actually slaughter her."

She half laughed. "I'll defend her. I'm driving over with Colin. I'll see you there, too."

"That's marvelous."

"Colin's out on the gallops just now. We're setting off after he's come in and had something to eat."

"Tell him to drive carefully. Tell him to think of Ambrose."

"Yes. . . . Isn't it awful about that crash?"

"Have you heard what happened, exactly?"

"Apparently, Ambrose tried to pass a slow lorry on a bend and there was another one coming the other way. He ran into it head on, and one of the lorries overturned and crushed another car with three stable lads in it. There's quite a lot about it in today's *Sporting Life*."

"I expect I'll see it. And, Midge . . . thank Colin for his message last night."

"I will. He said he didn't want you to worry any longer. He seemed to think you were almost as worried about her as we were."

"Almost," I agreed wryly. "See you at Warwick."

Chapter Fourteen

Honey had arranged for me to fly a Mr. and Mrs. Whiteknight and their two young daughters down to Lydd, where the daughters were to meet friends and leave on the car-air ferry to Le Touquet for a holiday in France. After waving the daughters off, the Whiteknights wanted to belt back to see their horse run in the first race at Warwick, which meant, since there was no racecourse strip, landing at Coventry and hailing a cab.

Accordingly, I loaded them up at Buckingham and pointed the nose of the Six toward Kent. The two daughters, about fourteen and sixteen, were world-weary and disagreeable, looking down their noses at everything with ingrained hostility. Their mother behaved to me with cool condescension, and autocratically bossed the family. Mr. Whiteknight, gruff, unconsulted, a downtrodden universal provider, out of habit brought up the rear.

At Lydd, after carrying the daughters' suitcases unthanked into the terminal, I went back to the Six to wait through the farewells. Mr. Whiteknight had obligingly left his *Sporting Life* on his seat. I picked it up and read it. There was a photograph of the Ambrose crash. The usual mangled metal, pushed to the side of the road, pathetic result of impatience.

I turned to the middle page to see how many races Colin was riding at Warwick. He was down for five, and in most of them was favorite.

Alongside the Warwick program, there was an advertisement in bold black letters.

"COLIN ROSS HAS INSURED WITH US. WHY DON'T YOU?" Underneath in smaller type, it went on, "*You* may not be lucky enough to survive two narrow escapes. Don't chance it. Cut out the proposal form printed below and send it with five pounds to the Racegoers' Accident Fund, Avon Street, Warwick. Your insurance cover starts from the moment your letter is in the post."

I put the paper down on my knee, looked into space, and sucked my teeth.

Major Tyderman had told Annie Villars that he and a partner of his had something going for them that would make them rich. She had thought he meant control of Rudiments, but of course it hadn't been that. The maneuvering with Rudiments had come about simply because Tyderman couldn't resist a small swindle on the side, even when he was engaged in a bigger one.

Tyderman had got Annie to introduce him to the Duke, so that he in his turn could produce Carthy-Todd. Goldenberg was incidental, needed only for placing bets. Carthy-Todd was central, the moving mind, the instigator. Everyone else, Tyderman, the Duke, Colin, Annie, myself—all of us were pieces on his chessboard, to be shoved around until the game was won.

Clean up and clear out, that was how he must have decided to play. He hadn't waited for the Fund to grow slowly and naturally; he'd blown up an airplane and used Colin Ross for publicity. He would only have stayed anyway until the claims began mounting, and if the crash victims at Newmarket were in fact insured he would be off within the week. He would stay just long enough to collect the crash-inspired rush of new premiums, and that would be that. A quick transfer to a Swiss bank. A one-way ticket to the next happy hunting ground.

I didn't know how to stop him. There would be no proof that he meant to defraud until after he'd done it. I could produce nothing to back up my belief. No one was going to lurch into drastic action on what was little more than a guess. I could perhaps telephone to the Board of Trade . . . but the Board of Trade and I were now hardly on speaking terms. The tall man might listen. He had, after all, once asked for my thoughts. Maybe the aircraft section had a hot line to the insurance section. And maybe not.

With a sigh, I folded up Mr. Whiteknight's newspaper and glanced again at the crash on the front page. Down in one corner in the left-hand column, beside the account of the accident, a paragraph heading caught my eye.

Tyderman, it said. I read the dry meager lines underneath with a vague and then mounting feeling of alarm.

"A man believed to be Major Rupert Tyderman was found dead early yesterday beside the main London to South Wales railway line, between Swindon and Bristol. His death, at first attributed to a fall from a train, was later established as having been the result of a stab wound. The police, who had wanted to interview Major Tyderman, are making inquiries."

The Whiteknight parents were walking back across the apron by the time I'd decided what to do. They were displeased when I met them and said I was going to make a telephone call. There wasn't time, they said.

"Check on the weather," I lied. They looked up at the hazy heat-wave sky and gave me deservedly bitter looks. All the same, I went on my way.

The Duke's polite manservant answered.

"No, Mr. Shore, I'm very sorry, His Grace left for Warwick half an hour ago."

"Was young Matthew with him?"

"Yes, sir."

"Do you know if he was planning to go to the Accident Fund office before he went to the racecourse?"

"I believe so, sir. Yes."

I put the receiver down, feeling increasingly fearful. Rupert Tyderman's death put the game into a different league. Lives had been at risk before, in the airplane; the basic callousness was there; but on those occasions the intention had been expressly not to kill. But now, if Carthy-Todd had decided to clear up behind him . . . if Tyderman's blunder with Nancy's airplane, which had led to his uncovering, had also led directly to his death . . . if Carthy-Todd had stopped Tyderman giving evidence against him . . . then would he, could he possibly, also kill the simple, honest, truth-spilling Duke? . . .

He wouldn't, I thought coldly. He couldn't.

I didn't convince myself one little bit.

The Whiteknights had no cause for complaint about the speed at which I took them to Coventry, though they consented only with bad grace when I asked to share their taxi to the races. I parted from them at the main gate and walked back toward the town center, looking for the office of the Accident Fund. As the Duke had said, it wasn't far: less than a quarter of a mile.

It was located on the first floor of a small moderately well-kept town house which fronted straight onto the pavement. The ground floor seemed to be uninhabited, but the main door stood open and a placard on the wall just inside announced, "Racegoers' Accident Fund. Please walk up."

I walked up. On the first landing there was a washroom, a secretary's office, and, at the front of the house, a door with a Yale lock and a knocker in the shape of a horse's head. I flipped the knocker a couple of times and the door came abruptly open.

"Hello," said young Matthew, swinging it wide. "Uncle was just saying you would miss us. We're just going along to the races."

"Come along in, my dear chap," said the Duke's voice from inside the room.

I stepped into the office. At first sight a plushy one: wall-to-wall plum-colored carpet, but of penny-pinching quality, two fat-looking easy chairs with cheap foam seats, a pair of shoulder-high metal filing cabinets, and a modern formica desk. The atmosphere of a solid, sober, long-established business came exclusively from the good proportions of the bay-windowed room, the moldings round the nineteenth-century ceiling, the carved wood and marble slab of the handsome fireplace, and some dark old gilt-framed oils on the walls. The office had been chosen with genius to convince, to reassure, to charm. And as clients of insurance companies seldom if ever visited its office, this one must have been designed to convince, to reassure, to charm only the Duke himself.

The Duke introduced me to the man who had been sitting and who now stood behind the desk.

"Charles Carthy-Todd . . . Matthew Shore."

I shook his hand. He'd seen me before, as I'd seen him. Neither of us gave the slightest sign of it. I hoped he had not distinguished in me the minute subsidence of tension which I saw in him. The tension I felt hadn't subsided in the slightest.

He was all the Duke had said: a man with good presence, good voice, a thoroughgoing public-school gent. He would have had to be, to net the Duke; and there were all those silver-framed photographs, which the Duke had mentioned, standing around to prove it.

He had dark hair with the merest sprinkling of gray, a compact little mustache, pinkish-tan slightly oily-looking skin, and heavy black-framed glasses assisting his grayish-blue eyes.

The Duke was sitting comfortably in an armchair in the bay window, his splendid head haloed by the shining day behind. His knees were crossed, his hands relaxed, and he was smoking a cigar. From his general air of pleased well-being, it was easy to see the pride he held in his beautiful benevolent Fund. I wished sincerely for his sake that he wasn't going to have to wake up.

191

Charles Carthy-Todd sat down and continued with what he had been going to do when I arrived, offering young Matthew a piece of chocolate-covered orange peel from a half-empty round red-and-gold tin. Matthew took it, thanked him, ate it, and watched him with anxious reserve. Like the Duke, I trusted young Matthew's instinct. All too clearly, it had switched to amber, if not to red. I hoped for all our sakes that he would have the good manners to keep quiet.

"Give Matthew a proposal form, Charles," the Duke said contentedly. "That's what he's come for, you know, to join the Fund."

Carthy-Todd obediently rose, crossed to the filing cabinet, pulled open the top drawer, and lifted out two separate sheets of paper. One, it appeared, was the proposal form; the other a lavishly curlicued certificate of insurance. I filled in the spaces on the ultra-simple proposal while Carthy-Todd inscribed my name and a number on the certificate; then I handed over a fiver, which left me with enough to live on cornflakes until payday, and the transaction was complete.

"Take care of yourself now, Matt," joked the Duke, and I smiled and said I would.

The Duke looked at his watch. "Good gracious!" He stood up. "Come along now, everybody. Time we went along to the racecourse. And no more excuses, Charles, I insist on you lunching with me." To me he explained, "Charles very rarely goes to the races. He doesn't much care for it, do you see? But as the course is so very close . . ."

Carthy-Todd's aversion to race meetings was to my mind completely understandable. He wished to remain unseen, anonymous, unrecognizable, just as he'd been all along. Charles would choose which meetings he went to very carefully indeed. He would never, I imagined, turn up without checking with the Duke whether he was going to be there, too.

We walked back to the racecourse, the Duke and Carthy-Todd in front, young Matthew and I behind.

Young Matthew slowed down a little and said to me in a quiet voice, "I say, Matt, have you noticed something strange about Mr. Carthy-Todd?"

I glanced at his face. He was half anxious, half puzzled, wanting reassurance.

"What do you think is strange?"

"I've never seen anyone before with eyes like that."

Children were incredibly observant. Matthew had seen naturally what I had known to look for.

"I shouldn't mention it to him. He might not care for it."

"I suppose not." He paused. "I don't frightfully like him."

"I can see that."

"Do you?"

"No," I said.

He nodded in satisfaction. "I didn't think you would. I don't know why Uncle's so keen on him. Uncle," he added dispassionately, "doesn't understand about people. He thinks everyone is as nice as he is. Which they're not."

"How soon can you become his business manager?"

He laughed. "I know all about trustees. I've got them. Can't have this and can't do that, that's all they ever say, Mother says."

"Does your uncle have trustees?"

"No, he hasn't. Mother's always beefing about Uncle not being fit to control all that lucre and one day he'll invest the lot in a South Sea bubble. I asked Uncle about it and he just laughed. He told me he has a stockbroker who sees to everything and Uncle just goes on getting richer and when he wants some money for something he just tells the stockbroker and he sells some shares and sends it along. Simple. Mother fusses over nothing. Uncle won't get into much trouble about money because he knows that he doesn't know about it, if you see what I mean?"

"I wouldn't like him to give too much to Mr. Carthy-Todd," I said.

He gave me a flashing look of understanding. "So

193

that's what I felt. . . . Do you think it would do any good if I sort of tried to put Uncle off him a bit?"

"Couldn't do much harm."

"I'll have a go," he said. "But he's fantastically keen on him." He thought deeply and came up with a grin. "I must say," he said, "that he has awfully good chocolate orange peel."

Annie Villars was upset about Kenny Bayst. "I went to see him for a few moments this morning. He's broken both legs and his face was cut by flying glass. He won't be riding again before next season, he says. Luckily he's insured with the Racegoers' Fund. Sent them a tenner, he told me, so he's hoping to collect two thousand pounds at least. Marvelous thing, that Fund."

"Did you join?"

"I certainly did. After that bomb. Didn't know it was Rupert then, of course. Still, better to do things at once rather than put them off, don't you agree?"

"Were Kitch and the stable lads insured, too, do you know?"

She nodded. "They were all Kitch's own lads. He'd advised them all to join. Even offered to deduct the premium from their wages bit by bit. Everyone in Newmarket is talking about it, saying how lucky it was. All the stable lads in the town who hadn't already joined are sending their fivers along in the next few days."

I hesitated. "Did you read about Rupert Tyderman in *Sporting Life?*"

A twinge of regret twisted her face: her mouth, for the first time since I had known her, took on a soft curve that was not consciously constructed.

"Poor Rupert. . . . What an end, to be murdered."

"There isn't any doubt, then?"

She shook her head. "When I saw the report, I rang the local newspaper down at Kemble—that's where they found him. He was lying, they said, at the bottom on an embankment near a road bridge over the railway. The local theory is that he could have been brought there by car during the night, and not fallen from a train at all. . . ." She shook her head in bewilderment. "He had one stab wound below his left shoulder blade, and he had been dead for hours and hours when he was found."

It took a good deal of lying in wait to catch the Duke without Carthy-Todd at his elbow, but I got him in the end.

"I've left my wallet in the Accident Fund office," I said. "Must have left it on the desk when I paid my premium. . . . Do you think, sir, that you could let me have a key, if you have one, so that I can slip along and fetch it?"

"My dear chap, of course." He produced a small bunch from his pocket and sorted out a bright new Yale. "Here you are. That's the one."

"Very kind, sir. I won't be long." I took a step away and then turned back, grinning, making a joke.

"What happens, sir, if it's you who gets killed in a car crash? What happens to the Fund then?"

He smiled back reassuringly, in a patting-on-the-shoulder avuncular manner. "All taken care of, my dear chap. Some of the papers I signed, they dealt with it. The Fund money would be guaranteed from a special arrangement with my estate."

"Did Charles see to it?"

"Naturally. Of course. He understands these things, you know."

Between the Duke and the main gate, a voice behind me crisply shouted.

"Matt."

I stopped and turned. It was Colin, hurrying toward me, carrying the saddle from the loser he'd partnered in the first race.

"Can't stop more than a second," he said. "Got to change for the next. You weren't leaving, were you? Have you seen Nancy?"

"No. I've been looking. I thought . . . perhaps . . ."

He shook his head. "She's here. Up there, on the balcony, with Midge."

I followed where he was looking, and there they were, distant, high up, talking with their heads together, two halves of one whole.

"Do you know which is Nancy?" Colin asked.

I said without hesitation, "The one on the left."

"Most people can't tell."

He looked at my expression and said with exasperation, "If you feel like that about her, why the bloody hell don't you let her know? She thinks she made it all up. . . . She's trying to hide it, but she's pretty unhappy."

"She'd have to live on peanuts."

"For crying out loud, what does that matter? You can move in with us. We all want you. Midge wants you—and now, not some distant time when you think you can afford it. Time for us is now, this summer. There may not be much after this." He hitched the saddle up on his arm and looked back toward the weighing room. "I'll have to go. We'll have to talk later. I came after you now, though, because you looked as though you were leaving."

"I'm coming back soon." I turned and walked along with him toward the weighing room. "Colin . . . I ought to tell someone . . . you never know . . ." He gave me a puzzled glance and in three brief sentences I told him why the Accident Fund was a fraud, how he and the bomb had been used to drum up business, and in what way Carthy-Todd was a fake.

He stopped dead in his tracks. "Good God," he said. "The Fund was such a great idea. What a bloody shame."

Saturday afternoon. The Board of Trade had gone home to its lawnmowing and the wife and kids. I put down the telephone and considered the police.

The police were there, on the racecourse, all ready

and able. But willing? Hardly. They were there to
direct the traffic; a crime not yet committed would
not shift them an inch.

Both lots, if they believed me, might eventually
arrive on Carthy-Todd's doorstep. By appointment,
probably; especially the Board of Trade.

There would be no Carthy-Todd to welcome them
in. No records. No Fund. Possibly no Duke ...

I always told myself to stay out of trouble.

Never listened.

No clocks ticked in Carthy-Todd's office. The
silence was absolute. But it was only in my mind that
it was ominous and oppressive. Carthy-Todd was safe
at the races and I should have a clear hour at least: or
so my brain told me. My nerves had other ideas.

I found myself tiptoeing across to the desk. Ridiculous. I half laughed at myself and put my feet down
flat on the soundless carpet.

Nothing on the desk top except a blotter without
blots, a tray of pens and pencils, a green telephone, a
photograph of a woman, three children, and a dog in
a silver frame, a desk diary, closed, and the red-and-
gold tin of chocolate orange peel.

The drawers contained stationery, paper clips,
stamps, and a small pile of the "insure against bombs
on the way home" brochures. Two of the four drawers
were completely empty.

Two filing cabinets. One unlocked. One locked.

The top of the three drawers of the unlocked cabinet
contained the packets of proposal forms and insurance
certificates and a packet of claim forms; the second
contained the completed and returned forms of those
insured, filed in a rank of folders from A–Z; and the
third, almost empty, contained three folders only, one
marked "Claims settled," one "Claims pending," and
one "Receipts."

"Claims settled" embraced the records of two separate outgoing payments of one thousand pounds, one
to Acey Jones and one to a trainer in Kent who had

been kicked in the face at evening stables. Three hundred pounds had been paid to a stable girl in Newmarket in respect of fracturing her wirst in a fall from a two-year-old at morning exercise. The claim forms, duly filled in and with doctor's certificates attached, were stamped "Paid," with a date.

"Claims pending" was fatter. There were five letters of application for claim forms, annotated "forms sent," and two forms completed and returned, claiming variously for a finger bitten off by a hungry hurdler and a foot carelessly left in the path of a plow. From the dates, the claimants had been waiting only a month for their money: and few insurance companies paid out quicker than that.

The thin file "Receipts" was in many ways the most interesting. The record took the form of a diary, with the number of new insurers entered against the day they paid their premiums. From sporadic twos and threes during the first week of operation, the numbers had grown like a mushroom.

The first great spurt was labeled in the margin, in small tidy handwriting, "A.C. Jones, etc." The second, an astronomical burst, was noted "Bomb!" The third, a lesser spurt, "Pamphlet." The fourth, a noticeable upthrust, "Electric failure." After that, the daily average had gone on climbing steadily. The word, by then, had reached pretty well every ear.

The running total in two months had reached 5,-472. The receipts, since some insurers had paid double premiums for double benefits, stood at £28,040.

With the next inrush of premiums after the Kitch-Ambrose accident (which Carthy-Todd certainly had not engineered, as only nonclaiming accidents were any good to him), there would have been almost enough in the kitty to settle all the claims. I sighed, frowning. It was, as Colin had said, a bloody shame. The Duke's view of the Fund was perfectly valid. Run by an honest man, and with its ratio of premiums to payoff slightly adjusted, it could have done good all round.

I slammed the bottom drawer shut with irritation

and felt the adrenalin race through my veins as the noise reverberated round the empty room.

No one came. My nerves stopped registering tremble; went back to itch.

The locked cabinet was proof only against casual eyes. I tipped it against the wall and felt underneath, and sure enough it was the type that worked on one connecting rod up the back: pushed the rod up from the bottom and all the drawers became unlocked.

I looked through all of them quickly, the noise I had made seeming to act as an accelerator. Even if I had all the time in the world, I wanted to be out of there, to be gone.

The top drawer contained more folders of papers. The middle drawer contained a large gray metal box. The bottom drawer contained two cardboard boxes and two small square tins.

Taking a deep breath, I started at the top. The folders contained the setting-up documents of the Fund and the papers which the Duke had so trustingly signed. The legal language made perfect camouflage for what Carthy-Todd had done. I had to read them twice, to take a strong grip and force myself to concentrate, before I understood the two covenants the Duke had given him.

The first, as the Duke had said, transferred one hundred thousand pounds from his estate into a guarantee trust for the Fund, in the event of his death. The second one at first sight looked identical, but it certainly wasn't. It said in essence that if the Duke died within the first year of the Fund, a further one hundred thousand pounds from his estate was to be paid into it.

In both cases, Carthy-Todd was to be sole trustee.

In both cases, he was given absolute discretion to invest or use the money in any way he thought best.

Two hundred thousand pounds. . . . I stared into space. Two hundred thousand pounds if the Duke died. A motive to make tongue-silencing look like child's play.

The twenty-eight thousand of the Fund money was

only the beginning. The bait. The jackpot lay in the dead Duke.

His heirs would have to pay. Young Matthew, to be precise. The papers looked thoroughly legal, with signatures witnessed and stamped, and in fact it seemed one hundred per cent certain that Carthy-Todd wouldn't have bothered with them at all if they were not foolproof.

He wouldn't waste much more time, I thought. Not with the claims for the Ambrose accident coming in. With the Duke dead, the two hundred thousand would have to be paid almost at once, because the covenants would be a first charge on his estate, like debts. There would be no having to wait around for probate. If Carthy-Todd could stave off the claims for a while, he could skip with both the Duke's money and the whole Fund.

I put the papers back in their folder, back in the drawer. Closed it. Gently. My heart thumped.

Second drawer. Large metal box. One could open it without removing it from the cabinet. I opened it. Lots of space, but few contents. Some cotton wool, cold cream, glue, and a half-used stick of grease paint. I shut the lid, shut the drawer. Only to be expected.

Bottom drawer. Knelt on the floor. Two small square tins, one seemed empty, one full and heavy and fastened all round with adhesive tape. Looked inside two cardboard boxes first and felt the breath go out of my body as if I'd been kicked.

The cardboard boxes contained the makings of a radio bomb. Solenoids, transmitters, fuse wire, a battery, and a small container of gunpowder in the first box. Plastic explosive wrapped in tin foil in the other.

I sat on my heels looking at the small square heavy tin. Heard in my mind the tall man from the Board of Trade: the tighter you pack a bomb, the more fiercely it explodes.

Decided not to open the small square tin. Felt the sweat stand out in cold drops on my forehead.

I shut the bottom drawer with a caution which

seemed silly when I remembered the casual way I'd tilted the whole cabinet over to open it. But then the bomb wouldn't go off until it got the right signal . . . and it wouldn't get the signal where it was, not with those precious documents in the cabinet just above.

I wiped my hand over my face. Stood up. Swallowed.

I'd found everything I came to find, and more. All except for one thing. I glanced round the office, looking for somewhere else. Somewhere to hide something big . . .

There was a door in the corner behind Carthy-Todd's desk which I assumed connected with the secretary's office next door. I went over to it. Tried the handle. It was locked.

I let myself out of Carthy-Todd's office and went into the secretary's room, whose door was shut but had no keyhole. Stared, in there, at an L-shaped blank wall. No connecting door to Carthy-Todd. It was a cupboard, with the door on his side.

I went back to Carthy-Todd's office and stood contemplating the door. If I broke it open he would know. If I didn't, I could only guess at what was inside. Evidence of a fraud was committed, which would spur the Board of Trade to action. Evidence that would make the Duke rescind his covenants, or at least rewrite them so that they were no longer death warrants. . . .

Carthy-Todd hadn't been expecting trouble. He had left the key to the cupboard on his desk in the tray of pens and pencils. I picked up the single key which lay there, and it fitted.

Opened the cupboard door. It squeaked on its hinges, but I was to engrossed to notice.

There he was. Mr. Acey Jones. The crutches, leaning against the wall. The white plaster cast lying on the floor.

I picked up the cast and looked at it. It had been slit neatly down the inside leg from the top to the ankle. One could put one's foot into it like a boot, with the bare toes sticking out of the end and the metal walking support under the arch. There were small grip clips like those used on bandages sticking into the plaster all down the opening. Put your foot into the cast, fasten the clips, and bingo, you had a broken ankle.

Acey Jones, loudy drumming up business for the Fund.

Acey Jones, Carthy-Todd. Confidence tricksters were the best actors in the world.

I didn't hear him come.

I put the cast back on the floor just where it had been, and straightened up and started to shut the cupboard door, and saw him moving out of the corner of my eye as he came into the room. I hadn't shut the office door behind me when I'd gone back. I hadn't given myself any time at all.

His face went rigid with fury when he saw what I'd seen.

"Meddling pilot," he said. "When the Duke told me he'd given you the key—" He stopped, unable to speak for rage. His voice was different, neither the Rugby of Carthy-Todd nor the Australian of Acey Jones. Just ordinary uninflected English. I wondered fleetingly where he came from, who he really was—a thousand different people, one for every crime.

Unblinking behind the black-framed glasses, the pale blue-gray eyes all but sizzled. The incongruous white eyelashes, which Matthew had noticed, gave him now a fierce, fanatical ruthlessness. The decision he was coming to wasn't going to be for my good.

He put his hand into his trouser pocket and briefly pulled it out again. There was a sharp click. I found myself staring at the knife which had snapped out, and thought with a horrific shiver of Rupert Tyderman tumbling down dead beside the railway line. . . .

He took a step sideways and kicked shut the office door. I twisted round toward the mantelshelf to pick up whatever I could find there—a photograph, a

202

cigarette box, anything I could use as a weapon or a shield.

I didn't even get as far as taking anything into my hand, because he didn't try to stab me with the knife.

He threw it.

Chapter Fifteen

It hit me in the left shoulder blade, and the jolt threw me forward on my twisting legs to that I hit my forehead solidly on the edge of the marble slab manstelshelf. Blacking out, falling, I put out a hand to stop myself, but there was nothing there, only the empty black hollow of the fireplace and I went on, right down, smashing and crashing among the brass fire irons ... but I heard them only dimly ... and then not at all.

I woke up slowly, stiffly, painfully, after less than a quarter of an hour. Everything was silent. No sound. No people. Nothing.

I couldn't remember where I was or what had happened. Not until I tried to get up. Then the tearing soreness behind my shoulder stung me straight back into awareness.

Had a knife sticking in my back.

Lying face down among the fire irons, I felt gingerly round with my right hand. My fingers brushed like feathers against the hilt. I cried out at my own touch. It was frightful.

Stupid the things you think of in moments of disaster. I thought: Damn it, only three weeks and one day to my medical. I'll never pass it. . . .

Never pull knives out of wounds, they say. It makes the bleeding worse. You can die from pulling knives out of wounds. Well . . . I forgot all that. I could see only that Acey-Carthy-Todd had left me for dead, and if he found me alive when he came back he would most certainly finish the job. Therefore I had to get out of his office before he came back. And it seemed incongruous, really, to walk round Warwick with a knife in one's back. So I pulled it out.

I pulled it out in two stages and more or less fainted after each. Kidded myself it was concussion from the mantelshelf, but I was crying as well. No stoic, Matt Shore.

When it was out, I lay where I was for a while, looking at it, snivelling weakly and feeling the sticky warmth slowly spread, but being basically reassured because I was pretty certain by then that the knife had not gone through into my lung. It must have hit my shoulder blade at an angle: it had been embedded to three or four inches, but slanting, not straight in deep. I wasn't going to die. Or not yet.

After a while, I got up onto my knees. I didn't have all the time in the world. I put my right hand on Carthy-Todd's desk; pulled myself to my feet.

Swayed. Thought it would be much worse if I fell down again. Leaned my hip against the desk and looked vaguely round the office.

The bottom drawer of the second filing cabinet was open.

Shouldn't be. I'd shut it.

Open.

I shifted myself off the desk and tried a few steps. Tottered. Made it. Leaned gingerly against the wall. Looked down into the drawer.

The two cardboard boxes were still there. The empty tin was still there. The small square heavy tin wasn't.

Realized coldly that the future no longer meant simply getting myself to safety out of that office, but getting to the Duke before the bomb did.

It was only four hundred yards. . . . Only . . .

I'd have to do it, I thought, because if I hadn't searched the office Carthy-Todd wouldn't now be in a tearing hurry. When I didn't turn up to ferry home the Whiteknights—or turn up anywhere again, for that matter, except with a stab wound in a ditch—the Duke would say where I had been last . . . and Carthy-Todd would want to avoid a police investigation like a slug shrinking away from salt. He wouldn't wait for that. He would obliterate my tracks.

There was something else missing from the office. I didn't know what it was, just knew it was something. It niggled for a moment, but was gone. Didn't think it could be important. . . .

Walked with deliberation to the door. Opened it, went outside. Stopped dead at the top of the stairs, feeling dizzy and weak.

Well. Had to get down them somehow. Had to.

The handrail was on the left-hand side. I couldn't bear to lift my arm. Turned round, hung on tightly, and went down backward.

"There you are," I said aloud. "You bloody can." Didn't convince myself. It took Carthy-Todd to convince.

I laughed weakly. I was a fully paid-up insurer with the Fund. Like to see Carthy-Todd pay my claim . . . a thousand smackers for a knife in the back. Lovely.

Rolled out into the hot sunlit street as lightheaded as a blonde.

Blond Acey Jones . . .

Acey Jones was being pushed. Hurried. Knowing I'd found him out but still believing he could retrieve the situation. Still make his two hundred thousand. If he kept his nerve. If he killed the Duke immediately, this afternoon, and somehow made it look like an accident. If he dumped me somewhere later, as he had the Major. . . .

He would think he could still do it. He didn't know I'd told Colin, didn't know that Colin knew he was Carthy-Todd. . . .

The empty street had got much longer during the afternoon. Also it wouldn't stay absolutely still. It shimmered. It undulated. The pavement was uneven.

207

Every time I put my foot down, the paving stones reached up and stabbed me in the back.

I passed only an elderly woman on the way. She was muttering to herself. I realized that I was, too.

Half way. I squinted along the gate of the car park. Had to make it. Had to. And that wasn't all. Had to find someone to go and fetch the Duke, so that I could explain ... explain ...

Felt myself falling and put a hand out toward the wall. Mustn't shut my eyes. . . . I'd be done for. . . . Spun heavily against the bricks and shuddered at the result. Rested my head against the wall, trying not to weep. Couldn't spare the time. Had to get on.

I pushed myself back into a moderately upright walking position. My feet couldn't tell properly how far it was down to the pavement: half the time I was climbing imaginary steps.

Weird.

Something warm on my left hand. I looked down. My head swam. Blood was running down my fingers, dripping onto the pavement. Looked up again, along to the course. Head swam again. Didn't know if it was concussion or heat or loss of blood. Only knew it reduced the time factor. Had to get there. Quickly.

One foot in front of the other, I told myself . . . just go on doing that: one foot in front of the other. And you'll get there.

Concentrate.

I got there. Gate to the car park. And no official guarding it. At that time in the afternoon, they'd given up expecting further customers.

I said, "Ohhh," in weak frustration. Have to go still further. Have to find someone. . . . I turned in to the car park. Through the car park there was a gate into the paddock. Lots of people there. Lots . . .

I went between the cars, staggering, holding on to them, feeling my knees bending, knowing the dizzy weakness was winning, and caring less and less about the jagged pain of every step. Had to find someone. Had to.

Someone suddenly called to me from quite close.

"Matt!"

I stopped. Looked slowly round. Midge was climbing out of Colin's parked Aston Martin down the row and running to catch me up.

"Matt," she said, "we've been looking for you. I came back to the car because I was tired. Where have you been?"

She put her hand with friendship on my left arm.

I said thickly, "Don't . . . touch me."

She took her hand away with a jerk. "Matt!"

She looked at me more closely, at first in puzzlement and then in anxiety. Then she looked at her fingers, and where she'd grasped my coat there were bright red smears.

"It's blood," she said blankly.

I nodded a fraction. My mouth was dry. I was getting very tired.

"Listen. . . . Do you know the Duke of Wessex?"

"Yes. But—" she protested.

"Midge," I interrupted. "Go and find him. Bring him here. . . . I know it sounds stupid . . . but someone is trying to kill him . . . with a bomb."

"Like Colin? But that wasn't—"

"Fetch him, Midge," I said. "Please."

"I can't leave you. Not like this."

"You must."

She looked at me doubtfully.

"Hurry."

"I'll get you some help, too," she said. She turned lightly on her heel and half walked, half ran toward the paddock. I leaned the bottom of my spine against a shiny gray Jaguar and wondered how difficult it would be to prevent Carthy-Todd from planting his bomb. That tin . . . it was small enough to fit into a binocular case . . . probably identical with the one which had destroyed the Cherokee. I would have sweated at the thought of so much confined explosive power if I hadn't been sweating clammily already.

Why didn't they come? My mouth was drier. . . . The day was airless. . . . I moved restlessly against the car. After I'd told the Duke, he'd have to go off

209

somewhere and stay safely out of sight until the
Board of Trade had dealt with Carthy-Todd. . . .

I dispassionately watched the blood drip from my
fingers onto the grass. I could feel that all the back of
my coat was soaked. Couldn't afford a new one, either. Have to get it cleaned, and have the slit invisibly
mended. Get myself mended, too, as best I could.
Harley wouldn't keep the job for me. He'd have to get
someone else in my place. The Board of Trade doc-
tors wouldn't let me fly again for weeks and weeks. If
you gave a pint of blood as a donor, they grounded
you for over a month. . . . I'd lost more than a pint
involuntarily, by the looks of things . . . though a pint
would make a pretty good mess if you spilled it. . . .

I lifted my lolling head up with a jerk. Got to stay
awake until they came. Got to explain to the Duke . . . .

Things were beginning to fuzz round the edges. I
licked my dry lips. Didn't do much good. Didn't have
any moisture in my tongue either.

I finally saw them, and it seemed a long way off,
coming through the gate from the paddock. Not just
Midge and the Duke, but two others as well. Young
Matthew, jigging along in front.

And Nancy.

Chanter had receded into the unimportant past. I
didn't give him a thought. Everything was as it had
been before, the day she flew to Haydock. Familiar,
friendly, trusting. The girl I hadn't wanted to get
involved with, who had melted a load of ice like an
acetylene torch.

Across the sea of cars, Midge pointed in my direction and they began to come toward me, crossing
through the rows. When they were only twenty or so
yards away, on the far side of the row in front of me,
they unaccountably stopped.

Come on, I thought. For God's sake, come on.

They didn't move.

With an effort, I pushed myself upright from the
Jaguar and took the few steps past its bonnet, going
toward them. On my left, six cars along, was parked
what was evidently the Duke's Rolls. On the bonnet

stood a bright red-and-gold tin. Matthew was point-ing, wanting to cross over and fetch it, and Midge was saying urgently, "No, come on, Matt said to come quickly, and he's bleeding. . . ."

Matthew gave her a concerned look and then nodded, but at the last second temptation was too much and he ran over and picked up the tin and started back to join them.

Bright red-and-gold tin. Containing sticks of orange peel dipped in chocolate. It had been on the desk. And afterward . . . not on the desk. Something miss-ing. Red-and-gold tin.

Missing from Carthy-Todd's desk.

My heart bumped. I shouted, and my voice came out hopelessly weak.

"Matthew, throw it to me."

He looked up doubtfully. The others began to walk through the row of cars toward him. They would reach him before I could. They would be standing all together, Nancy and Midge and the Duke and young Matthew, who knew, too, that I'd been in Carthy-Todd's office that day.

I scanned the car park desperately, but he was there. He'd put the tin on the car and simply waited for them to come out of the races. The last race was about to start . . . the horses had gone down to the post and at that moment the loudspeakers were an-nouncing, "They're under starter's orders". . . . He knew it wouldn't be long before they came. . . . He was standing over nearer the rails of the course, with his black head showing and the sun glinting on his glasses. He had meant just to kill young Matthew and the Duke, but now there were Nancy and Midge as well . . . and he didn't know he couldn't get away with it . . . didn't know Colin knew . . . and he was too far away for me to tell him. . . . I couldn't shout . . . could barely talk.

"Matthew, throw me the tin." It was a whisper, nothing more.

I began to walk toward him, holding out my right arm. Stumbled. Swayed. Frightened him.

211

The others were closing on him.

No more time. I took a breath. Straightened up.

"Matthew," I said loudly. "To save your life, throw me that tin. Throw it now. At once."

He was upset, uncertain, worried.

He threw the tin.

It was taking Carthy-Todd several seconds to press the transmission buttons. He wasn't as adept at it as Rupert Tyderman. He wouldn't be able to see that he had missed his opportunity with the Duke, and that now there was only me. But whatever he did, he'd lost the game.

The red-and-gold tin floated toward me like a blazing sun and seemed to take an eternity crossing the fifteen feet from Matthew. I stretched my right arm forward to meet it, and when it landed on my hand I flung it with a bowling action high into the air behind where I was standing, back as far as I could over the parked rows, because behind them, at the rear, there was empty space.

The bomb went off in the air. Three seconds out of my hand, six seconds out of Matthew's. Six seconds. As long a time as I had ever lived.

The red-and-gold tin disintegrated into a cracking fireball like the sun, and the blast of it knocked both young Matthew and me with a screeching jolt flat to the ground. The windows in most of the cars in the park crashed into splinters, and the two Fords just below the explosion were thrown about like toys. Nancy and Midge and the Duke, still sheltered between two cars, rocked on their feet and clung to one another for support.

Along in the stands, we heard later, no one took much notice. The race had started and the commentator's voice was booming out, filling everyone's ears with the news that Colin Ross was lying handy and going nicely on the favorite half a mile from home.

Young Matthew picked himself up smartly and said in amazement, "What was that?"

Midge completed the four steps to his side and held his hand.

"It was a bomb," she said in awe. "As Matt said, it was a bomb."

I was trying to get myself up off the grass. Even though the Duke was for the present safe, the Fund money was not. Might as well try for set and match. . . .

On my knees, I said to Matthew, "Can you see Carthy-Todd anywhere? It was his tin . . . his bomb. . . ."

"Carthy-Todd?" repeated the Duke vaguely. "It can't be. Impossible. He wouldn't do a thing like that."

"He just did," I said. I was having no success in getting up any further. Had nothing much left. A strong arm slid under my right armpit, helping me. A soft calm voice said in my ear, "You look as if you'd be better staying down."

"Nancy. . . ."

"How did you get into this state?"

"Carthy-Todd . . . had a knife. . . ."

"There he is!" Matthew suddenly shouted. "Over there."

I wobbled to my feet. Looked where Matthew was pointing. Carthy-Todd, running between the rows. Nancy looked, too.

"But that's," she said incredulously, "that's the man I saw in the car with Major Tyderman. I'd swear to it."

"You may have to," I said.

"He's running to get out," Matthew shouted. "Let's head him off."

It was almost a game to him, but his enthusiasm infected several other racegoers who had come early out of the races and found their windows in splinters.

"Head him off," I heard a man shout, and another, "There, over there. Head him off."

I leaned in hopeless weakness against a car, and dimly watched. Carthy-Todd caught sight of the growing number converging on him. Hesitated. Changed course. Doubled back on his tracks. Made for the only free and open space he could see. The green grass behind him. The racecourse itself.

"Don't. . . ." I said. It came out a whisper, and even if I'd had a microphone he wouldn't have heard.

"Oh, God," Nancy said beside me. "Oh, no."

Carthy-Todd didn't see his danger until it was far too late. He ran blindly out across the course, looking over his shoulder at the bunch of men who had suddenly, aghast, stopped chasing him.

He ran straight in front of the thundering field of three-year-olds sweeping round the last bend to their final flying effort up the straight.

Close-bunched, they had no chance of avoiding him. He went down under the pounding hoofs like a rag into a threshing machine, and a second later the flowing lines of horses broke up into tumbling chaos . . . crashing at thirty miles an hour . . . legs whirling . . . jockeys thudding to the ground like bright blobs of paint . . . a groaning shambles on the bright green turf. . . . And side-stepping, swaying, looking over their shoulders, the rear ones in the field swerved past and went on to a finish that no one watched.

Nancy said in anguish "Colin!" and ran toward the rails. The pink-and-white silks lay still, a crumpled bundle curled in a protective ball. I followed her, plod by plod, feeling that I couldn't go any farther, I simply couldn't. One car short of the rails, I stopped. I clung on to it, sagging. The tide was going out.

The pink-and-white ball stirred, unrolled itself, stood up. Relief made me even weaker. Crowds of people had appeared on the course, running, helping, gawping, closing in like a screen round the strewn bodies. . . . I waited for what seemed an age, and then Colin and Nancy reappeared through a thronging wall of people and came back toward the car park.

"Only stunned for a second," I heard him say to a passing inquirer. "I shouldn't go over there . . ." But the inquirer went on, looking avid.

Nancy saw me and waved briefly, and ducked under the rails with Colin.

"He's dead," she said abruptly. She looked sick.

"That man—he—he was Acey Jones. . . . Colin said you knew—his hair was lying on the grass—but it was a wig—and there was this bald white head and that pale hair—and you could see the line of grease paint—and the black mustache. . . ." Her eyes were wide. Full of horror.

"Don't think about it," Colin said. He looked at me. "She shouldn't have come over. . . ."

"I had to—you were lying there," she protested. He went on looking at me. His expression changed. He said, "Nancy said you were hurt. She didn't say how badly." He turned abruptly to Nancy and said, "Fetch the doctor."

"I tried to before," she said. "But he said he was on duty and couldn't see to Matt before the race in case he was needed. . . ." She tailed off and looked over at the crowd on the course. "He'll be over there, seeing to those two jockeys. . . ." She looked back at Colin with sudden fright. "Midge said Matt had cut his arm. . . . Is it worse? . . ."

"I'll fetch him," Colin said grimly, and ran back to the battlefield. Nancy looked at me with such flooding anxiety that I grinned.

"Not as bad as all that," I said.

"But you were walking. . . . You threw that bomb with such force . . . I didn't realize. . . . You do look ill."

The Duke and young Matthew and Midge reappeared from somewhere. I hadn't seen them come. Things were getting hazier.

The Duke was upset. "My dear chap," he said over and over again. "My dear chap. . . ."

"How did you know it was a bomb?" Matthew asked.

"Just knew."

"That was a pretty good throw."

"Saved our lives," said the Duke "My dear chap. . . ." Colin was back.

"He's coming," he said. "Immediately."

"Saved our lives," said the Duke again. "How can we repay . . ."

Colin looked at him straight. "I'll tell you how, sir. Set him up in business . . . or take over Derrydowns . . . give him an air-taxi business, based near Newmarket. He'll make you a profit. He'll have me for a customer, and Annie, and Kenny . . . and in fact the whole town, because the Fund can go on now, can't it?" He looked at me inquiringly, and I fractionally nodded. "It may cost a bit to put it right," Colin said, "but your Fund can go on, sir, and do all the good it was meant to. . . ."

"An air-taxi business. Take over Derrydowns," the Duke repeated. "My dear Colin, what a splendid idea. Of course. Of course."

I tried to say something . . . anything . . . to begin to thank him for so casually thrusting the world into my fingers . . . but I couldn't say anything . . . couldn't speak. I could feel my legs collapsing. Could do nothing any more to stop them. Found myself kneeling on the grass, keeping myself from falling entirely by hanging on to a door handle of the car. Didn't want to fall. Hurt too much.

"Matt!" Nancy said. She was down on her knees beside me. Midge, too. And Colin.

"Don't bloody die," Nancy said.

I grinned at her. Felt lightheaded. Grinned at Colin. Grinned at Midge.

"Want a lodger?" I asked.

"Soon as you like," Colin said.

"Nancy," I said. "Will you . . . will you . . ."

"You nit," she said. "You great nit."

My hand slipped out of the door handle. Colin caught me as I fell. Everything drifted quietly away, and by the time I reached the ground I couldn't feel anything at all.